THE SEARCH
FOR THE
SILVER EAGLE

BY ED DUNLOP

The Search for the Silver Eagle
By Ed Dunlop

Cover illustration by Regie Milburn
Copy Editor: Julia C. Hansen
Proofreaders: Anita Nish and Katie Krueger

Published by
PACE Publications
Independence, MO 64055

Printed in the United States of America
Set in Times New Roman 12 point
ISBN 0-918407-05-2

DEDICATION

To the kids and workers at
Calvary Independent Baptist Church,
who became such a precious
part of my life.

"Ye that fear the Lord,

trust in the Lord:

he is their help and their shield"

Psalm 115:11

Contents

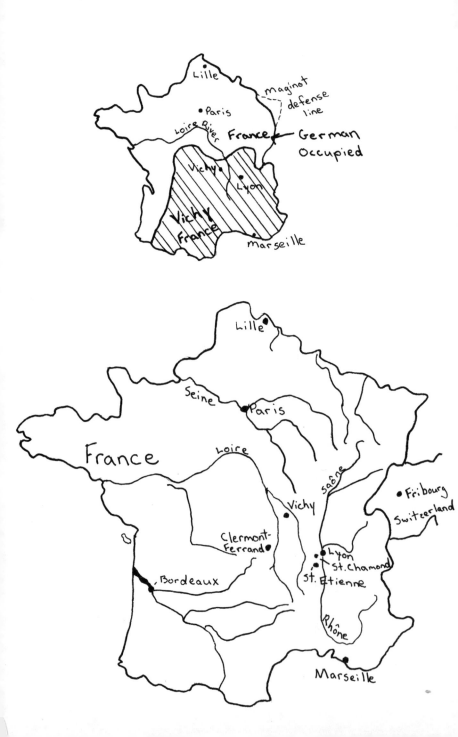

Historical Note

Vichy France

World War II began with Germany's invasion of Poland on September 1, 1939. France and Great Britain declared war on Germany just two days later.

The Germans invaded France on May 12, 1940, and entered Paris on June 14. France signed an armistice with Germany on June 22, allowing the Germans to occupy the northern two-thirds of France while southern France remained under French control.

Southern France, governed by Henri Philippe Petain from the capital city of Vichy became known as Vichy France. In November 1942, German troops seized and occupied Vichy France.

1

FLIGHT

"Hans! Watch out!"

Hans looked up just in time to see that the falling tree was about to crush him to the earth. There was no time to run. He hurled his axe to one side and dropped to the ground beside the fallen tree he had been trimming.

The huge shagbark hickory came crashing down on top of him. The ground shook with the impact.

Hans lay motionless for a moment beneath the tree, then took a deep breath. He let it out slowly. "That was close!"

"Hans! Are you all right?"

"*Ja*, I'm fine, Papa!" Hans replied. "But I can't move! My legs are pinned to the ground."

"I'll have you out in a second," Papa promised, scrambling through the branches until he reached Hans. He carried a huge, two-man crosscut saw. "I'm sorry, Son," Papa said as he attacked a branch. "I thought she was gonna fall uphill. At the last second, the wedges slipped and—well, thank the Lord you weren't killed!"

Papa sawed furiously. "That was quick thinking, dropping behind the log like that. You could have been flattened."

Moments later, the thick branch dropped lower against Hans as the saw severed it from the trunk. Papa dropped the saw and dragged the branch clear. Hans crawled out from under the tree and noted the tears streaking his father's face. "If you have something against me, Papa . . ."

Herr Kaltenbrünner laughed, then grabbed Hans and hugged him. "Oh, Hans, I'm sorry! Thank God you weren't killed! Are you sure you're all right?"

"*Ja,* I'm fine, Papa, really I am. A bit shook up, but I'm fine."

Herr Kaltenbrünner was a man of medium height and build, but had the broad shoulders and thick hands of a man accustomed to rugged outdoor work. A thick brown mustache accented his friendly face and sandy brown hair.

Hans, his twelve-year-old son, was tall and slim, with wiry strength not usually found in a youth of his age. He brushed the dry leaves out of his blond hair. His intense blue eyes sparkled with love for his father.

He smiled as he stepped over to retrieve the axe. Something moving below in the valley caught his attention. "Look, Papa!"

High on the mountainside where Hans and his father were cutting firewood, they were afforded a panoramic view of most of Fribourg Valley. As the Kaltenbrünners watched, a black automobile far below sped up the steep mountain road, barely slowing for the winding, treacherous curves.

"He's really in a hurry, isn't he?" Hans said. "I hope he makes that next curve!"

The car disappeared from view as the road dipped behind the crest of a hill. Moments later, the speeding vehicle flashed into view, slowed, then turned into the steep, narrow lane leading up to the Kaltenbrünner chalet.

Papa frowned. "He's going to the chalet!"

"Papa, that's a Nazi automobile!" Hans shouted. "And Gretchen's in the chalet alone!" Dropping their woodcutting tools, father and son dashed frantically down the hillside toward the chalet.

The black car skidded sideways as it came to a stop in the driveway below the chalet. The passenger door flew open and a large, red-faced man leaped out. "It's Colonel Von Bronne!" Hans exclaimed in amazement, "the Allied agent who helped us escape from Austria!"

"*Herr* Kaltenbrünner!" the colonel called. "Come down! Bring Hans and Gretchen! Hurry!"

Fear swept over Hans as he rushed up the chalet steps to find his sister. The desperate tone in the colonel's voice indicated that danger was at hand. As Hans and Gretchen reached the car, Colonel Von Bronne seized the door handle and threw the back door open. "Quickly!" he gasped. "Get in! There isn't time to explain!"

The startled family scrambled into the back seat as the colonel leaped into the front. Even as Papa slammed the door closed, the auto lurched in reverse, showering the side of the chalet with flying gravel. The car then leaped forward and sped down the steep lane. Alarmed, Hans leaned over and saw Lieutenant Hofer at the wheel.

"Colonel, what's this all about?" Papa asked with a note of concern in his voice. "Where are you taking us?"

"We have reason to believe that the *Gestapo* may have located you," the gray-haired colonel answered, as he scanned Fribourg Valley with a heavy pair of binoculars.

"But that's impossible!" Hans' father exclaimed.

"We thought so, too," the colonel answered, "but one of our agents intercepted a communication with your names and the mention of the town of Fribourg. If the *Gestapo* has not located you, it is getting mighty close!"

Colonel Von Bronne suddenly stiffened. "Lieutenant! Go back the way we came! There's a military motorcar heading this way, and he'll be up with us in less than a minute!"

Hans was thrown against the door as Lieutenant Hofer braked, and the heavy car skidded sideways across the road. The engine roared as the lieutenant accelerated, and the powerful car shot forward. Moments later, they were taking the curves so fast that the tires screamed in protest. "Slow down!" Gretchen wailed.

"Take the road to the west," the colonel ordered as the road intersected another. With a screech of brakes and a roar from the engine, the limousine fishtailed dangerously and then swung onto the smaller road. The lieutenant floored the accelerator, and the trees lining the road became a blur.

"There's another motorcar down below us!" Papa called, and Hans pressed his nose to the window. The road far below angled up the side of the mountain toward them. Hans saw another black car speeding in their direction.

"If that road intersects this," the colonel said, "and that motorcar contains *Gestapo* agents, they'll have us in half a minute!"

The limousine careened into a sharp curve, then swept down into a dip in the road. Lieutenant Hofer braked hard. Dust and smoke poured from the rear tires as the car screeched to a stop at the side of the road. "Everyone out!" the lieutenant shouted, even before the car stopped. "I'll drive on as a decoy!"

The four passengers tumbled from the car and ran for the woods. The lieutenant gunned the engine and continued down the road alone. Hans saw the colonel draw a shiny automatic from his coat. *Herr* Kaltenbrünner leaped over a fallen log and dropped to the ground behind it. "Over here!" he called. "Here's a quick hiding place!"

Hans dropped into place beside his father, and Gretchen and the colonel ducked right behind him. Seconds later, with a screech of protesting tires and the roar of exhaust, the other car sped by in pursuit of the limousine.

Colonel Von Bronne groaned aloud. "That was the *Gestapo*, all right. Just as we feared." Hans winced at these words.

The colonel leaped to his feet. "Keep moving!" he ordered. "We've got to find a place to hole up until Lieutenant Hofer can catch up with us and we can come up with a plan of action."

He led the way into the shadowy forest, and the others followed. Hans prayed as he brought up the rear. "Help us, Lord," he whispered. "If the Nazis really have found us, where do we go now?"

Ten minutes later, Colonel Von Bronne stopped. He held up one hand as a signal for silence as he stood motionless in the shadow of a tall fir. His keen eyes scanned the hillside. Finally, he turned to the Kaltenbrünners. "This might be a good place," he told them. "Follow me, but stay alert and watch for trouble."

The colonel led the way through a clearing to a ruined farmhouse. The roof and two outer walls had collapsed, resulting in a twisted pile of decaying planks and shingles. The fugitives carefully picked their way through the ruins until the colonel located the door to a cellar. As he descended into the darkness, the colonel carefully tested each step in the rotting staircase to be certain that it would support his weight. The others followed him and found themselves in the gloom of a musty cellar illuminated dimly by two dirt-caked windows.

"Stay here until I return," the colonel told Papa. "I think this is as safe a place as any, but we can't take any chances." He drew his handgun and handed it to Papa. "Know how to handle a Walther automatic?"

Papa nodded as he slipped the Walther into his waistband. "I can stop a Nazi or two if I have to."

"But this is Switzerland!" Hans protested. "The Nazis aren't allowed to touch us here!"

Colonel Von Bronne shook his head. "*Nein.* The fact that Switzerland is neutral will not stop a *Gestapo* hit squad from kidnapping or killing you. Now that we know that they are on your trail, we must get you out of the country."

Gretchen burst into tears. "But we've just been here for three weeks," she sobbed. "I don't want to spend the rest of my life running from the Nazis!" Hans stepped close and put his arm around her.

The colonel smiled grimly. "It won't be like last time," he assured Gretchen. "My agents and I helped Jacob and his father escape to America, and we will find a place of safety for you."

He drew a second gun. "I'll find Lieutenant Hofer and then come back for you," he promised. "You're relatively safe here. Stay put until I come for you. If I'm not back before nightfall, this is a good place to spend the night. But I'm hoping to return before dark."

As the colonel left, Gretchen sank to a seat on a stack of old lumber. "Why are the Nazis still looking for us?" she wailed. "I thought we were safe once we left Austria!"

Her father sat beside her and pulled her close. "When you and Hans helped Jacob escape from Austria with the documents, you exposed a number of Nazi double agents and revealed the locations of several top-secret munitions factories. The Germans aren't likely to forgive and forget, you know."

"I am glad we did it," Gretchen declared, "for Austria, and 'cause the Nazis killed Mama!"

Her father nodded. "I'm proud of you and Hans for what you did for Austria," he replied. "But now that we know that the *Gestapo* is still searching for you, we all know we are in danger. We'll have to trust the Lord for protection and pray that Colonel Von Bronne can find a safer home for us."

They sat in silence for several minutes, each alone with his thoughts.

Gretchen looked up at her father. "Papa," she asked, "do you still miss Mama?"

Papa nodded slowly. "I guess I still think about her just about every moment of every day," he replied. His eyes welled up with tears, and he hugged Gretchen tighter. "It's been almost four months since the Nazi planes strafed our village, but the pain of losing your mother hasn't lessened. I suppose it will always be this way."

Papa smiled sadly, and playfully pulled one of his daughter's long, blond braids. "I see your mother every time I look at you, Sweetheart. I suppose she must have looked just like you when she was nine years old."

He wiped his eyes with the back of a calloused hand. "There are times, Gretchen, when I just can't . . ." His voice failed as he choked back a sob.

Hans leaned against him and squeezed his shoulder. "Mama's in heaven, Papa," he said gently, "with Jesus."

☽ ☽ ☽

It was nearly midnight when Hans awoke. His heart raced as footsteps sounded above the cellar. Silently he reached over and shook his father's arm. "Papa, wake up!" he whispered urgently. "Someone's coming!"

His father drew the automatic from his belt and cocked the action quietly. The door creaked as a dark figure appeared at the top of the flight of stairs. In the dim moonlight Hans could see his father quietly aim the weapon.

"Kaltenbrünner!" a voice whispered urgently. "Don't shoot!"

Papa lowered the automatic. Relief flooded over Hans as he realized that the intruder was Colonel Von Bronne. The colonel hurried forward. "I have bad news," he told them in a voice tinged with emotion. "Lieutenant Hofer was killed in a gun battle with the *Gestapo* agents."

2

ESCAPE

"Let's stop and take a rest," Colonel Von Bronne said as he leaned against an outcropping of granite to catch his breath. "I think we're traveling a little too fast for Gretchen."

"I can keep up!" Gretchen panted as she scrambled up the steep slope. "Just because I'm a girl doesn't mean that you have to wait for me!"

The colonel laughed. "Don't take it personally, Gretchen. Actually, I'm the one who needs the rest." In spite of the cold November air, he pulled a huge handkerchief from his pocket and wiped the perspiration from his face. "These old legs aren't what they used to be."

"Colonel," *Herr* Kaltenbrünner said, "you haven't told us much. Where are we heading? What are your plans for us?"

Colonel Von Bronne reached inside his greatcoat and withdrew a sheaf of papers. "I'm sorry," he apologized. "I was so anxious to get moving that I haven't taken the time to explain."

"Here." He handed the papers to Hans' father. "These are your Austrian passports, prepared by an Austrian magistrate who just happens to be an Allied agent. You'll notice that I took the liberty of providing you with a name change."

"What!" Hans exclaimed. "You mean that Papa is no longer Hans Kaltenbrünner?"

The big colonel laughed. "I'm afraid not, Hans. From now on, he's Gustav Von Edler. It's a precaution we're taking to make it more difficult for the *Gestapo* to track you. You and Gretchen also have new names. Your name is now Hans Von Edler, and your sister is Gretchen Von Edler."

"Gretchen Von Edler," Gretchen repeated. "That's different. I like it."

"We're taking other precautions, too," Von Bronne explained. "Several of my agents are creating false trails for the *Gestapo* to follow. But we're going further than that. We're doing everything we can to break every link in the chain that leads to you so that the Nazis will have no way to track you down.

"I'll take you as far as the French border and then turn you over to one of our most trusted agents. He won't even know your identities. Once you are safely in his hands, he'll take you to an unknown location in France. Even I won't know where you are, so there will be no way for the *Gestapo* to track you."

"France?" the new Gustav Von Edler repeated. "But France is occupied by German forces!"

The colonel shook his head. "*Nein*, not the entire country, just the northern two-thirds. We're sending you to Vichy, France, which is the southern sector still under French government."

"But why France?" Hans' father argued. "We're going directly toward German occupied territory instead of away from it!"

"Exactly. Hopefully, we're doing just the opposite of what the *Gestapo* anticipates. It's risky, but we're trying to place you in a location where the *Gestapo* least expects to find you."

Hans' father pocketed the crucial papers. "All right. I guess it does make sense—in a roundabout sort of way."

The colonel stood to his feet. "We have to move on. Less than two kilometers north of here we'll cross the southern lines of the Basel-Stadt Railway. There's a westbound freight due to pass in less than an hour, and it slows to a crawl by the time it crosses over Salnier Pass. Less than fifteen kilometers-per-hour, we were told. We'll attempt to hop aboard a boxcar there and ride the rails to the French border."

Hans frowned. "Jumping on a moving train sounds hard. Do you think Gretchen can make it?" Hans had watched over Gretchen ever since they were little, and he was concerned for her now.

"It's risky," the colonel replied. "But we'll help Gretchen. It's the fastest way we know to leave the country without leaving a trail for the *Gestapo* to follow."

*** *** ***

An hour later the four fugitives crouched in the brush on the bank above the railway. "When will that train get here?" Gretchen asked. "We've been waiting forever!"

Her father laughed. "Be patient, Sweetheart. We've only been here five minutes."

"It seems longer than that!"

"Sure it does—especially since it's so cold. But the train will come. Just be patient."

Hans stood up. "I think I hear it now!"

Colonel Von Bronne tugged at Hans' coat. "Stay down, Hans! We have to keep out of sight until the engines pass."

Moments later, the blazing headlight of the train cut through the darkness as it swept around the bend. Hearts pounding, the colonel and the three Von Edlers crouched even lower. The roar of the engines was deafening as the train thundered past, shaking the ground beneath their feet.

Hans watched the train. "It's going too fast!" he whispered. "It must be doing forty!"

"*Ja,*" the colonel replied, "but it's slowing down. By the time the engines reach the crest of the ridge, they'll be doing less than twenty. We'll try to board a car toward the rear of the train."

The colonel rose to his feet and slid down the embankment. "Come on, let's be ready! As soon as the train slows down, your father and I will try to get a cargo door open!"

The rails groaned and clacked as the long line of heavy freight cars rolled up the steep grade. Hans stood in the gravel of the right-of-way, watching as the engines labored to pull their load to the summit. He decided that they were indeed slowing down. Perhaps this would be easy after all.

"This one's unlocked!" Papa called, and Hans spun around to see his father clinging to the side of a boxcar. "Help me slide the door open!"

Colonel Von Bronne ran alongside the slowing boxcar, gripped the bottom of the huge door with both hands, and lunged forward. The door slid open, just a crack. Hans' father placed the bottom of one boot against the opening and shoved with all his might. The opening widened to just over a meter. Papa swung his body inside, then knelt in the opening, gripping the side of the door with his left hand.

"Gretchen first!" he shouted. "Sweetheart, just run alongside the car. I'll pull you in!"

Following her father's instructions, Gretchen ran alongside the open boxcar. Hans was relieved to see his sister's legs disappear through the doorway as her father jerked her inside. "You're next, Hans! Do it just like Gretchen! I'll pull you in!"

Hans started running. Ignoring his father's instructions, he leaped forward and grabbed the side of the door with both hands, then swung his legs upward through the doorway. The boxcar suddenly lurched forward, causing Hans to lose his handhold on the door. He fell heavily to the gravel of the railroad bed, landing on his back and striking his head on one of the wooden ties. Dazed by the fall, Hans was unaware that his right leg lay directly in the path of the huge iron wheels at the rear of the boxcar.

Strong hands gripped the collar of his coat and jerked him out of the path of the moving train. Hans felt himself being lifted to his feet. "Catch up with the boxcar, boy!" the colonel roared in his ear. "Your papa is a strong man. Let him pull you in!"

Moments later, Hans lay on the cold floor of the boxcar. His heart pounded as he tried to catch his breath. Colonel Von Bronne dropped in beside him.

Hans felt a hand on his shoulder and looked up to see his father's face silhouetted in the moonlight from the open door. "You all right, Son?"

Hans nodded. "*Ja,* Papa."

"Doing it your way almost cost you your life, Hans. If Colonel Von Bronne hadn't reacted in time, you would have at least lost a leg, maybe even been killed."

Hans nodded miserably. "*Ja,* Papa. I—I'm sorry."

"We won't mention it again, but I'll expect you to remember next time. Always follow instructions. Come on, let's get this door closed."

Once the door was secured, the fugitives rode in dark silence for several minutes. Hans relived his near tragedy, realizing how close he had come to death or crippling injury. He bowed his head and thanked God for sparing him through the quick actions of the colonel.

Gretchen's voice broke through the solitude of his thoughts. "It's cold in here."

Her father groped over to where her voice came through the darkness. "It's gonna get colder, Sweetheart. We'll have to huddle together for warmth."

"Maybe not," the colonel replied. "You'll never believe what this cargo is! It seems that we're in a boxcar loaded with hundreds of canvas tents! We'll just burrow into a stack of tents for warmth."

The four fugitives clambered to the top of a stack of tents in the corner and arranged a sleeping place under several layers of the thick canvas. As warmth returned to their tired bodies, the rhythmic clacking of the wheels on the rails lulled them to sleep.

Hans awoke to find that the train had stopped. The gray light of dawn streamed through an open door. Alarmed, Hans looked over to his left. The colonel was gone!

Hearing voices, Hans crept to the edge of the stack of tents and peered down in time to see two armed soldiers slip silently into the boxcar. One glance at the green uniforms with the red and black armbands told him that these were Nazi soldiers!

3

CLOSE CALL

Holding his breath, Hans quietly crept back from the edge of the stack of tents, then began to crawl across the top of the cargo. *Father, please don't let them find us!* he prayed in desperation. The sound of heavy boots told him that one of the Nazi soldiers was directly below him.

"I'll search down here," one of the soldiers called to his companion. "Why don't you crawl up on top and take a look?"

"What are we looking for?" the other man asked.

"Fugitives, I guess," the first voice answered. "My, was that station master hot! Said we had no right to search a Swiss train." He laughed. "But Lieutenant Dusselmetz convinced him differently."

Hans safely reached the spot where his father and Gretchen lay sleeping. He reached down and shook them gently. "Wake up!" he whispered urgently. "Two Nazi soldiers are searching the boxcar! We have to hide!"

A low, barely audible scratching sound caught his attention, and he looked over to see Colonel Von Bronne's head and shoulders protruding from the space between two stacks of canvas. "Over here!" the colonel whispered. "Hurry!"

Hans followed Gretchen into the cavern that the colonel had created, and their father dropped in behind them. Colonel Von Bronne pulled several layers of canvas over the opening, then wedged his body beneath them to hold them in place should one of the soldiers step on that spot.

Buried under layers of tents, Hans prayed fervently. He could hear one of the Nazis moving about as he searched the top of the stacks of canvas. At one point, he felt tremendous pressure as the man walked over their hiding place.

"There's nobody in here," the soldier down below finally called. "Let's move on to another car!" Hans heard the welcome sound of the door sliding shut.

Fifteen minutes later, as the train began to move, Hans' father slid from his hiding place. "Stay put," he told the others. "I'll check it out." Moments later he pulled the layers of canvas open to reveal their hiding place. "Come on out," he said softly. "The Nazis are gone!"

Late that afternoon the train screeched to a stop. Colonel Von Bronne peered through the crack between the doors. "Villeurbanne" he read. "Here's where we get off! Welcome to France."

He tried the door. "It's locked from the outside! We'll have to wait until someone opens it."

The fugitives waited in silence for nearly an hour. Suddenly, a loud metallic clank echoed through the boxcar. "Stay close to me," the colonel whispered, "and don't say anything!"

Sunlight splashed into the boxcar as a worker slid the door open. "Excuse us, please," Colonel Von Bronne said pleasantly as he stepped quickly past the startled cargo handler. He walked briskly across the cargo platform with Hans, Gretchen, and their father hurrying to keep up. As they rounded the corner of the building, Hans cast a quick glance over his shoulder. The cargo handler was standing motionless beside the open door of the boxcar, staring after them with his mouth open.

They hurried into the woods behind the station. "Our agent is supposed to meet us somewhere in the vicinity of the station," the colonel told them. "Stay here until I make contact with him."

He was back in half an hour. "Well, this is it," he said, shaking hands with Papa, then Hans, and then Gretchen. "*Auf Wiedersehen*. God be with you. Take the street directly across from the depot, and one block down you'll come to a sidewalk café. Your man is in an old automobile parked at the curb. He's wearing a dark green topcoat. Just get into the auto without saying anything, and he'll take it from there. I'll follow from a distance to see that you reach the auto safely. *Auf Wiedersehen*."

"*Danke schön*, Colonel," Hans said.

Colonel Von Bronne put a hand on Hans' shoulder, and his other hand on Gretchen's. "*Danke schön* to both of you," he said quietly, "for all you did for Austria!" He walked away quickly.

The French agent turned out to be a young, dark-haired man with a thin face and a sparse mustache. "Call me Pierre," he told the Von Edlers as he drove them out of town. "That's not my real name, of course, but the less we know about each other, the better."

As he reached the city limits, Pierre stepped hard on the accelerator, and the old car surged ahead. "I'm taking you to St. Chamond, about a hundred kilometers southeast of the capital city of Vichy," he explained. "St. Chamond is a city of about ten thousand people, nestled in a valley between the Forez and Vivarais mountain ranges. South of St. Chamond is the little village of Messiere. We think we have a place for you—on a farm just outside of Messiere, owned by an elderly couple named Dubois. Their barn burned down recently, and you and your son can help *Monsieur* Dubois rebuild the barn in return for your room and board."

Papa nodded. "It sounds like a workable situation." He looked over at Gretchen and Hans. "Time to brush up on our French, *oui*?"

Silver moonlight streamed across an empty cornfield as Pierre's car chugged noisily up the narrow lane leading to the Dubois farm. A feeling of apprehension swept over Hans as he and the others got out of the car to stand before the darkened farmhouse. The front door of the house opened abruptly, and a tall, frail-looking man carrying a lantern stepped out on the porch.

"Monsieur Dubois," Pierre greeted him, "we have a family of displaced persons that need a place to stay. We thought that perhaps . . . "

"Bring them in!" the elderly farmer interrupted. "Our door is always open!" He held the lantern higher. "Who are they?"

"A family of three, from Switzerland," Pierre replied. "That's all I know. But the man and the boy will make able workers for the reconstruction of your barn."

"That will be a blessing indeed,*" Monsieur* Dubois said. He swung the lantern in Papa's direction. "Bring your things inside. We can give you the room on the east end of the house."

Papa cleared his throat. *"Merci, Monsieur.* We are grateful for your hospitality. But we have nothing to bring in, because all of our things were left behind."

The tall farmer nodded. "I understand. I'm sorry."

Papa turned to thank Pierre, but the auto was already speeding down the lane toward town. He put his arms around Hans and Gretchen, and together they followed their host into the house.

"My wife Anne is already asleep,*" Monsieur* Dubois whispered, "so I will show you to your room. You will meet her at breakfast, *oui*?"

The next morning, Hans awoke to the smell of breakfast cooking. His father's bed was empty, so Hans woke Gretchen, and together they hurried into the kitchen. Papa was seated at the kitchen table in deep discussion with *Monsieur* Dubois, and a large, gray-haired woman was busy at the cook stove.

The woman turned as Hans and Gretchen entered, then dropped a serving fork and hurried over to them. Her wrinkled face looked tired and strained, but her eyes twinkled with warmth and friendliness. "Let me look at you, young ones," she said. "*Monsieur* has told me all about you, but I must see for myself." She looked them both up and down, then turned back to their father. "*Oui, Monsieur* Von Edler, they are beautiful! You must be very proud!"

Papa smiled. "*Merci, Madame.* I am very proud. God has been good to me."

"But the children have no mother," *Madame* Dubois observed. "My heart goes out to you, young ones!" She patted Gretchen on the shoulder. "Well, sit at my table. I'll have breakfast on *tout de suite.*"

After breakfast, the woman took a two-franc coin from an earthenware jar and handed it to Hans. "Would you help an old woman and run into town for some sugar? It's less than a kilometer. If the mercantile is out, then borrow some from *Madame* Favier. She lives in the stone house across from the mercantile."

Gretchen leaped to her feet. "May I go, too, Papa? May I?"

"I think you should stay and help *Madame* with the dishes," Papa replied. "There'll be another time for a trip to town."

"Oh, let her go, *Monsieur*," their hostess laughed. "There'll be another time for helping with the dishes."

4

COLETTE DUVAL

"Doesn't this remind you of our little village of Mittersill?" Gretchen asked as she and Hans paused in the narrow lane overlooking the peaceful little town. She sighed suddenly. "Hans, I sometimes wonder if we'll ever see Austria again."

Hans squeezed her hand. "Sure we will, Gretchen. Papa says that the war will be over by this time next year. Once the Nazis are defeated, everything will return to normal, and we can go home again."

From their vantage above the town, Messiere looked like a cluster of tiny dollhouses left outside by a careless child. The neat white buildings extended across an emerald green valley and climbed the slopes of the mountains on each side. It was as though someone had tried to squeeze the town into an area that was just too small, and the buildings had spilled over on both sides. In the center of town, the tall spire of a church rose above the brown roofs.

"How do we find the mercantile?" Gretchen asked.

"*Madame* Dubois said to turn left at the second street," Hans answered. "That's easy enough."

Hans and Gretchen hurried along the cobblestone street. Gretchen wrapped her shawl closer about her. "It sure is cold." She suddenly stopped. "Hans, look at that girl!"

Across the narrow street, a tall, sturdily built girl stood at the corner of a two-story stone building. As Gretchen and Hans watched, the girl picked up a stone from the street and hurled it furiously. "Why don't you look where you're going?" she screamed. "You big, dumb ox!" She hurled another rock. "You are so stupid! Can't you watch out for other people?"

The building kept Gretchen and Hans from seeing the person with whom the girl was so upset, but a boy about her age stood nearby. "Colette, calm down!" he called. "It's as much your fault as his."

Colette gave the boy a venomous look. "Keep out of this, Philipe!" She picked up another rock. "Better watch yourself next time, Klause!" She hurled the rock, then bent over for another.

"Let's find out what's going on," Hans said, darting across the street. Gretchen was right on his heels. As they rounded the corner of the building, they saw to their amazement that the object of the girl's wrath was a huge man dressed in a dirty, tattered overcoat. He was bareheaded in spite of the cold, and his hair was dirty and matted. As Colette mocked and tormented him, the man made little moaning, sobbing sounds. Saliva drooled from his mouth into his thick, brown beard.

"Colette, stop it!" Philipe shouted. "Leave Klause alone! He's not hurting you!"

"I'd like to see him try!" Colette retorted. She raised her hand to throw her next rock.

A window opened just above them, and a small, bald-headed man with a huge white mustache leaned out. "Colette Duval," the man called, "drop that stone this instant and leave poor Klause alone! You ought to be ashamed of yourself, young lady!"

Colette looked up in defiance. "I don't have to obey you, *Monsieur* Jayet! You're just an ignorant Frenchman! And you're not a very good clock-maker!"

"I'm warning you, Colette—if I have to come down there, I'll whip your backside!"

"You wouldn't dare!"

"I'd dare," *Monsieur* Jayet replied, "and I'll do it! Your mother will thank me one day. I'm coming down right now!" The little man slammed the window and disappeared.

The girl realized that her bluff had been called. She paused uncertainly, turned, and hurled the rock at the window, and then dashed down the street. The missile bounced harmlessly off the stone wall.

Philipe turned to face the big man. "I'm sorry, Klause. I know you can't hear me, but I wish I could tell you that I'm sorry." The retarded man cowered away from Philipe, then crept away, still sobbing.

Philipe advanced timidly toward Hans and Gretchen. "*Bonjour*," Hans said. "I'm Hans Von Edler, and this is my sister Gretchen."

"I'm Philipe," the other boy said. "Philipe Duval. I'm sorry for the way Colette acted."

Hans was surprised. "Duval? Then Colette is your sister!"

Philipe nodded. "I'm afraid so."

"Who was that big, retarded man?" Hans asked Philipe.

"His name is Klause," Philipe answered. "He's deaf. Some unkind people around here call him the village idiot. A lot of kids are afraid of him, but he'd never hurt anybody. He cuts wood for people of the village in exchange for food."

"Where does he live?" Gretchen asked. "I feel sorry for him."

"He lives alone in the forest," a man's voice answered, and the three young people looked over to see *Monsieur* Jayet standing nearby. "Klause just appeared here in Messiere one day a few months ago," the man explained. "No one knows where he came from, but some folk think that perhaps he was a soldier who was gassed or shell-shocked. In fact, we don't even know what his name is, but someone started calling him 'Klause,' and the name stuck."

"Why was your sister so hateful to him?" Gretchen asked Philipe.

Philipe sighed. "I think Colette hates everybody now that Papa's gone." He suddenly held up one hand as if to wave good-bye. "Look, I've got to get home. It's been nice to meet you."

As Philipe walked away, *Monsieur* Jayet looked after him and shook his head. "Nice lad, Philipe Duval. It's a shame his sister isn't more like him."

"Why does she act the way she does?" Hans asked. The little man seemed friendly, and Hans felt at ease talking to him.

"She's been carrying on this way for the past six months," *Monsieur* Jayet answered. "She hates anything that has to do with France or being French. Her father was a munitions expert, and was working for the French government when he was killed in an accidental explosion. Apparently another worker detonated explosives before he was supposed to, and *Monsieur* Duval was killed as a result. Colette has allowed her hatred of France to grow to the point that she insists that she would rather be in Nazi Germany."

Hans frowned. "That girl doesn't know what she's saying!"

The little clock-maker shrugged. "Well, enough of Colette! And who are you two?"

"I'm Hans Von, uh, Von Edler," Hans replied, "and this is my sister, Gretchen."

"It's good to meet you," the friendly little man replied. "I'm *Monsieur* Jayet, the best and only clock-maker in Messiere. My wife runs the village inn downstairs, and my shop is upstairs, along with our living quarters. Stop in and see me sometime if you're interested in seeing what goes on inside a clock. And now, I suppose I had better get back to work."

"He was really nice, wasn't he?" Gretchen commented as they hurried to the mercantile for the sugar.

Hans nodded. "*Monsieur* Jayet makes up for the rudeness of Colette Duval."

Late that afternoon, Hans was helping his father and *Monsieur* Dubois lay out lumber for the new barn. The three looked up from their work to see a man racing a horse down the lane. "Did you hear the news?" the horseman shouted as he reined in beside the lumber pile. "The Nazis have invaded!"

Hans' father dropped a heavy beam and hurried over to the man. "Invaded, *Monsieur*? What do you mean?"

"I mean, *Monsieur*, that northern France wasn't enough for those murdering devils! Now Hitler has decided that he wants the region of Vichy France as well! An armored column marched into Messiere just two hours ago, tanks, artillery and all!"

The rider let out a discouraged sigh. "That's not the worst of it! The Nazi commanding officer decided that he wanted *Monsieur* Jayet's inn and shop as his headquarters. When *Monsieur* Jayet tried to resist, they shot him dead!"

5

DOGFIGHT

"Papa," Hans asked that evening in the privacy of their own room, "where will we go now? Is there any place that's safe from the Nazis?"

"Our best course is to stay where we are," Papa decided. "I'm sure that the borders are now closed. If we try to leave, we'll be stopped and questioned."

"But the soldiers are everywhere!" Gretchen declared. "What if they find out who we are?"

"There's no way for them to know that you and Hans were sought by the *Gestapo*," Papa replied. "You have new names. If you are ever questioned, simply say that we left Austria after your mama was killed accidentally in a strafing. It's the simple truth, and we'll trust God to keep them from learning the rest."

Fear settled over the peaceful village of Messiere like a blanket of fog on a cool morning. An entire division of Nazi troops occupied the town, and *Monsieur* Jayet was not the only one to lose property. The commanding officer moved a number of residents from their homes to quarter his troops, and those who dared resist or express disapproval were shot.

The presence of the Nazi troops was a daily insult. The soldiers seized every opportunity to question and harass the citizenry. They raided farms and stole livestock, killing or destroying anything they did not care to steal. Fear and frustration became a daily part of life.

The only one who welcomed the invasion was Colette Duval. She made no secret of the fact that she was delighted that the Nazis were now in control. When a farmer tried to save his livestock by moving them to a distant location, it was Colette who turned him in. Gretchen's disgust and mistrust of the girl increased.

On the third morning after the invasion, Hans made a cautious trip into town to do an errand for *Madame* Dubois. As he passed by the inn now serving as the Nazi headquarters, he paused, thinking about the friendly little clock-maker. He wondered what had happened to *Madame* Jayet.

Klause appeared, making odd little groaning noises as he shuffled down the street with a load of firewood strapped to his broad back. Hans watched in surprise as the strange woodcutter opened the door of the Nazi headquarters and carried his load inside.

A passerby noticed Hans' interest in the deaf man. "Klause has a new job cutting wood for the Nazi troops," he told Hans. "They're giving him food and lodging as payment. He no longer has to sleep in the woods."

Hans raised an eyebrow. "I'm surprised that they would show any kindness, even to a poor soul like Klause."

"Oh, I'm sure it's not a matter of kindness," the man replied. "They'll work that poor creature to death. I suppose the Nazi commander figures there's no danger of Klause overhearing any military secrets, since he's deaf and all."

Hans started to turn away, but the stranger seemed inclined to talk. "It's a shame what they did to *Monsieur* Jayet, is it not?"

Tears threatened to fill Hans' eyes as he answered, "I know. I just met him once, but he seemed like a good man."

"He was," the man agreed. "*Monsieur* Jayet was a saint. What angers me was the way they got him to tell them the combination to his safe. I heard that they're using the safe to keep their valuables and military papers."

"What did they do?" Hans asked.

"They threatened to shoot *Madame* Jayet unless her husband told them the numbers. Once they had the combination, they shot him because he complained about the seizure of his property."

"What happened to his wife?" Hans asked.

"I understand that she fled to another village to live with her brother." The man shook his head. "War is a terrible thing, lad."

"*Oui, Monsieur*, it is," Hans agreed. He hurried away.

Hans completed his errand and headed for home. As he walked up the lane leading from the village, he heard a shout. "Hans! Wait for me!"

Hans turned and saw Philipe running toward him. "Hans," Philipe said, panting to catch his breath, "How about going on a hike with me? There's an old mining camp about a kilometer from here. I'd like to show it to you. I think we can get there without running into any Nazi troops."

"I have to work on the barn all morning with Papa and *Monsieur* Dubois," Hans told him.

"Then we'll go this afternoon."

Hans hesitated.

"Colette won't come," Philipe assured him. "I won't tell her what we're going to do."

"Would you mind if Gretchen comes along? I think she would enjoy the outing."

Philipe nodded agreeably. "Sure. What if we meet in front of the bakery at two o'clock?"

The drone of engines drowned out Hans' reply, and both boys looked up to see a squadron of fighter planes flying over. "Those are British Spitfires!" Philipe said excitedly. "They have Rolls Royce Merlin III engines with a top speed of five hundred and two kilometers per hour."

Hans stared at him. "How do you know that?"

Philipe flipped open the small notebook he was carrying to reveal simple sketches of airplanes. "I draw the silhouettes of any new planes I see and ask around until somebody identifies them for me. It's just a hobby. I know most of the planes in the air today."

He frowned. "I wonder what the British were doing in this region."

Hans shrugged. "I have to hurry back, Philipe. See you at two. I'm looking forward to it."

That afternoon, Gretchen and Hans hurried into town to find Philipe sitting on the front steps of the bakery. "What's the rope for?" Hans asked, eyeing the coil of rope over Philipe's shoulder.

"There's a good climbing cliff just below the mining camp," Philipe answered. "I thought we might do some climbing and rappelling."

"I'm glad your big sister didn't come," Gretchen said, and Hans looked at her reproachfully.

"She's not my big sister," Philipe replied. "I hate to admit it, but actually, we're twins. We're both twelve."

"Twins!" Hans exclaimed. "Your sister is half a head taller than you! And she looks older."

"Girls mature faster than boys," Gretchen said sweetly.

"*Oui*, the lower life forms usually do," Philipe told her.

Gretchen stared at him. "What?"

"Amoebae mature faster than fruit flies," Philipe said. "Fruit flies mature faster than frogs; frogs mature faster than girls; and girls mature faster in some ways than boys. Like I said, the lower forms of life do mature faster."

Gretchen could think of nothing to say, so she stuck her tongue out at Philipe.

Philipe laughed. "Come on, you two, let's hike to the mining camp."

The roar of planes passing overhead caught his attention, and he shaded his eyes as he glanced upwards. "French fighters," he declared. "Nine of them." He squinted against the bright sunlight. "Looks like they're Bloch MB 152s! They have a top speed of five hundred twelve, and they carry two twenty-millimeter cannons and two 7.5mm machine guns."

"French fighters?" Hans questioned. "I thought all of France was taken over by the Nazis."

"These are probably Free French," Philipe explained, "resistance fighters who went underground when the Nazis took over, and now are returning to strike back. They're flying awfully low—probably not much more than a thousand meters or so."

"Look at that silver plane!" Hans called. "It looks like it has two fuselages!"

The silver plane had two long, slender fuselages connecting the wings with the tail section, with an engine mounted in the nose of each fuselage. Between the fuselages, the cabin of the aircraft extended from the front of the wing halfway back to the tail section, giving it a short, stubby appearance. It was as though the aircraft's designer had started building a third fuselage and then suddenly quit before he reached the tail.

Philipe studied the unusual aircraft. "That's an American plane!" he exclaimed. "It's a Lockheed P-38 Lightning. That's called a 'twin boom' design. It looks a bit strange, but they say it's a fast, efficient fighter. It carries four guns and two cannons in the nose." Philipe wrinkled his nose. "I wonder where he came from, and why he's flying with the French."

Hans watched as the squadron of green planes passed overhead, followed by the American plane. He saw movement out of the corner of his eye and looked over to see a formation of charcoal-gray planes diving toward the French squadron. "Philipe, look!" He pointed. "What are those?"

"German fighters!" Philipe exclaimed. He squinted against the bright sunlight. "Messerschmitts! Their top speed is well over six hundred, and they carry two twenty-millimeter cannons and two MG17 machine guns. The French fighters are in for a tough time!"

He groaned as the French squadron disappeared behind the mountain ridge. "There's gonna be a dogfight, and we won't get to see any of it!"

But as he spoke, the French squadron reappeared in a tight turn, climbing fast in a desperate attempt to gain altitude. "They've spotted the Messerschmitts," Philipe declared.

"We may get to see the fight, after all," Gretchen said.

Philipe nodded. "But it may not be much of a fight," he replied. "It's twelve against nine, and the Messerschmitts have a definite speed advantage."

Just then eight of the German planes came snarling down in a power dive directly toward the French squadron. At what seemed the last possible second, the group of attacking planes split into two formations and banked past the green French planes. The chatter of machine gun fire reverberated across the valley as the German pilots thumbed the trigger buttons on their control sticks.

But the French planes were no longer clustered in a tight formation. Diving, turning, climbing, twisting, they had scattered in evasive maneuvers just before the first volley was fired.

"The French planes may be slower," Philipe explained, "but they're more maneuverable than the Messerschmitts."

The French planes were now firing back at the Germans. The battle was in full swing, and the skies seemed filled with diving, twisting, and climbing aircraft. The snarl of straining engines combined with the chatter of machine guns and the deeper growl of cannons to create a thundering confusion of sound.

Two German planes bore down on the tail of a French fighter. The French pilot threw his plane into a twisting dive to throw his pursuers off his tail, but the Messerschmitts stayed with him, guns blazing, until the green plane erupted in smoke and spiraled toward the ground.

"Bail out! Bail out!" Philipe cried, as if the stricken pilot could hear him. But the falling plane disappeared behind the ridge, and the three young people knew that the pilot had been killed.

"Watch the American!" Hans cried. The silver fighter came screaming into a power dive toward a cluster of four Messerschmitts, then spat out three quick bursts from its cannon. One of the German planes went spiraling down in smoke and flames, then exploded just before it dropped behind the mountain. A second Messerschmitt began to leave a trail of dense, black smoke before it went into a wide turn and retreated from the battle.

"Two Germans down, one Frenchman down," Philipe reported. "The score now stands at ten to eight."

As the dogfight continued to rage above the village, the young people were delighted to see another gray Nazi plane go down. A white parachute popped open, and the downed pilot drifted right into the center of Messiere to land behind the church. Moments later, a green plane began to pour out smoke and left the battle in an attempt to limp back to its base.

"Nine to seven," Philipe said.

In the next few moments, the silver American plane shot down two more Messerschmitts. "How's he doing that?" Philipe remarked. "It seems that every time he gets his sights on an enemy plane, they go down in flames!"

Hans pointed. "*Oui*, but he's in trouble now!"

Several of the gray Messerschmitts had circled to gain altitude, then came diving toward the American with their guns and cannons blazing. The silver P-38 went screaming into a frantic dive. Twisting and turning, the American pilot maneuvered for his life, but the enemy planes managed to stay on his tail, pouring lead into the retreating plane the entire time.

"Come on, come on," Hans coaxed. "Out run them!"

The young people heard a muffled explosion, then saw a burst of orange flame erupt just forward of the P-38's cockpit. "He's on fire!" Philipe whispered tersely.

The dying plane spiraled toward the mountainside above them. Hans was relieved to see a white parachute open, then drift down toward the tree line as the burning plane disappeared somewhere above them on the mountain.

Philipe looked at Hans. "It looked like he went down close to the mining camp! Let's go see if we can find him! Maybe he needs help!"

"Philipe, look!" Gretchen pointed toward the Nazi headquarters. A Nazi officer and several other soldiers scrambled hurriedly into two jeeps and sped toward them, then slowed to negotiate the turn. "I want that American!" the officer shouted. "Take him dead or alive!"

"They saw the American pilot go down!" Philipe said frantically. "Hans, we have to get to him first! The Nazis will kill him!"

6

RESCUE ATTEMPT

"Hans! We have to find the American! We must get to him before the Nazis do!" Philipe was so overwhelmed by what he had just witnessed that his voice trembled. "Come with me, Hans! I know a shortcut!" Philipe ran between two buildings and scrambled up a steep mountain trail.

"Gretchen!" Hans shouted. "Get Papa! Tell him what happened! Have him get some men to search for the pilot! I'm going with Philipe!" He dashed after his friend.

Hans ran as hard as he could over the rough ground, dodging bushes and leaping over rocks in an attempt to catch up with Philipe. He stumbled and fell, slamming his elbow against a rock. Ignoring the pain, he leaped to his feet and ran even harder.

Hans caught up with his friend as Philipe was fighting his way through a ravine choked with a tangle of briars and dense undergrowth. "Work your way straight up the mountainside until you reach the crest of the first ridge," Philipe shouted. "I'll circle around toward the mining camp and work my way toward you. Watch for a white parachute!"

Hans fought his way through the brambles until he came to a clearing. A narrow dirt lane led up the side of the mountain, and Hans began to follow it. The going was now much easier. He scanned the trees for any sign of the American's parachute, but found nothing.

Hearing the sound of an engine, Hans looked back. A jeep was speeding up the trail toward him. He dived into the underbrush and lay still until it passed. Apparently, the soldiers hadn't seen him.

Ten minutes later, Philipe caught up with him again on the top of the ridge. "Find anything, Hans?"

Hans shook his head. "Nothing. I almost got run over by one of the jeeps. But I don't think they saw me."

"I searched the area around the mining camp, but saw no sign of a parachute. Let's work our way further up the mountain."

At that moment two Nazis crossed the ridge less than ten meters from where Hans and Philipe stood. The Germans were as surprised as the boys were. Hans turned to run, but one of the soldiers swung his submachine gun around and yelled, "Halt!"

Hans froze.

"What are you boys doing here?" the other soldier barked.

"W-we saw a p-parachute c-come down in the f-forest," Hans stammered. "W-we thought we'd t-try to find it."

"Go back to the village," the soldier ordered. "You have no business being here, and we had better not find you up here again."

Hans and Philipe hurried down through the thick undergrowth until they were out of sight of the Germans. Philipe stopped and retied his boot. "Let's cut around to the north, then work our way back up toward the top."

Hans stared at him. "You heard what the soldier said. We're not supposed to be on the mountain."

Philipe stood to his feet and gave Hans a look of contempt. "So you take orders from the enemy now?"

"No," Hans replied, "but they had machine guns, and they told us to . . . "

"They're the enemy, remember?" Philipe hissed. "I don't know about you, but I don't take orders from any Nazi! Come on, Hans, we've got to find that pilot before the soldiers do!"

The boys continued down the mountainside for another thirty or forty meters in case the German soldiers could see them, ran north several hundred meters, and then began to work their way back toward the top. The autumn leaves made a pleasant crunching sound underfoot, but both boys realized that the sound would betray their presence to any troops that happened along.

"We have to hurry; we have to hurry," Philipe kept repeating. "We have to find him before the soldiers do!"

They came to a rocky bluff nearly fifteen meters high that ran laterally across the face of the mountain. "This ledge runs for nearly half a kilometer in both directions," Philipe told Hans. "We'll have to climb it, or we'll lose too much time trying to go around."

Hans watched as Philipe started up the face of the bluff. Philipe moved slowly, deliberately, always checking to be sure that a handhold or foothold was secure before he trusted it with his full weight. Watching the careful, yet confident way Philipe climbed, Hans decided that his friend knew what he was doing. Hans gave him a three-meter head start, then tried to follow the same route that Philipe was taking.

Three minutes later, Hans gratefully crawled over the top and sank to the ground. "Give me just a minute to catch my breath," he told Philipe. "That was scary!"

"All right, but you can't rest too long," Philipe replied. "We have to keep going."

He suddenly held up one hand. "Listen!"

The crunch, crunch, crunch of autumn leaves warned that someone was coming! Both boys dropped face down in the leaves and flattened themselves to the ground. Two soldiers and an *unteroffizier* hurried past, unaware of the two boys hiding less than five meters away.

"That was close!" Hans whispered when the Nazis had passed. Philipe just nodded.

They hurried upwards, sliding into jagged ravines and scrambling up the other side, fighting their way through brambles and tangled undergrowth, clambering over giant boulders and fallen trees. An idea suddenly occurred to Hans, and he grabbed the back of Philipe's coat to get his attention. "You know what we should have done when we started?" he asked. "We should have prayed and asked God to help us in our search."

Philipe nodded slowly.

Hans bowed his head and prayed aloud. "Father, help us to find this American pilot before the Germans do! They'll kill him, Lord! If he's hurt badly, help him to recover. And Lord, help us to know where to hide him and how to get him out of here safely. In Jesus' name, Amen."

Hans wasn't sure exactly how his friend would respond to the idea of praying, but when Hans said "Amen," Philipe said it, too.

They struggled uphill for another ten minutes. "There's no way we're going to find him in time," Philipe said, "unless God does guide us to him."

Hans glanced back down the mountainside. "We've come quite a ways," he said. His heart leaped. A large patch of white was visible through the trees below! He pointed it out to Philipe.

"Let's go!" Philipe exulted.

The boys scrambled excitedly toward the object, which was less than a hundred meters away. But as they got close, Philipe stopped in dismay. "It's just a rock face reflecting the sun," he said. "Let's work our way further south as we go up."

Moments later, as Hans snake-crawled under a dense thicket, he heard a strange noise. He stopped and listened. Then he heard it again—a low moaning sound, as if a human were in tremendous pain.

"Philipe, wait!" he called.

Philipe squirmed around to face him. "What is it, Hans?"

"Listen!" Hans told him.

The groaning sound was repeated. "Come on," Philipe said eagerly. "It sounds like it's coming from just above us!" He scrambled through the briars and leaped to his feet.

"Hans, look!"

Hans jumped to his feet and looked upward. High overhead, the snow-white silk of a parachute canopy billowed in the upper branches of a tall sycamore. Dangling from the twisted shroud lines with his boots ten meters above the hillside was the motionless form of the American pilot!

Hans stared at the helmeted figure in the torn and bloody khaki uniform. "Is he dead?"

"Of course not!" Philipe snorted. "You heard him groan, didn't you?" He ran to the base of the tree. "How are we going to get him down? The soldiers could come along here at any minute!"

"Do you have a knife?" Hans asked.

"*Oui,* but . . ."

"Give it to me."

Philipe handed him the knife. "Hans, you can't just climb up and cut him down! He'll be killed in the fall. It looks like his legs got hit and may be broken."

"How long is your rope?" Hans asked.

"Huh?" Philipe had forgotten the line coiled around his shoulder. "Oh, the rope. It's forty meters."

"That's enough." Hans held out his hands. "Give me your rope. I'll climb the tree, tie the pilot off and then cut him free. Once I climb down, we can both lower him to the ground."

Philipe ducked out of the coil of rope. "But hurry, Hans!"

Both boys froze with fear as the rustling of leaves announced that someone was coming. "We can't hide," Philipe whispered. "They've seen the parachute, anyway."

To the relief of both boys, Gretchen burst from the undergrowth. She stared up at the unconscious pilot. "You found him!"

"Gretchen!" Hans whispered. "How did you get here?"

"After Papa left to get help, I just followed a dirt road up the mountain," Gretchen answered. "I saw the parachute in the tree and came down to it. I didn't know you were already here."

"You can help," Hans told her. "But we have to hurry."

Hans draped the coil over his shoulder and began to climb. Moments later, he was at eye level with the unconscious flier. "I think you're right, Philipe. Both his legs are bruised and swollen. He'll be in tremendous pain when he comes to."

Hans drew the knife from his pocket and cut a three-meter length from the end of the rope. He quickly tied one end around his own waist, then tied the other to a branch above him. Gripping one end of the longer rope in his left hand, he tossed the coil up and over a sturdy branch above the American and watched in satisfaction as the end fell unobstructed all the way to the ground. He slipped the knife back into his pocket.

Hans leaned out against the safety harness he had fashioned for himself, passed the end of the long rope through the pilot's parachute harness, and then tied a square knot. "I'm ready to cut him down," he called softly to Philipe and Gretchen. "Wrap your end of the rope around that sapling behind you. Be sure to take all the slack out of the line, then wrap it around three times and hold it."

"I'll just tie it off."

"No," Hans argued. "It'll be faster if you just wrap it around the trunk and hold the end."

"I don't think we can hold his weight, Hans."

"You don't have to!" Hans replied. "The friction of the rope around the tree will do that. If you've done some rappelling you ought to know that! Once I've cut him free, I'll come down and help you lower him to the ground."

"All right, it's ready," Philipe replied.

Hans leaned out again and sawed at the first parachute shroud line. "This stuff is tough! How many of these lines are there—twenty-eight?"

It took nearly ten minutes to cut through all the lines, and to the three young people it seemed like an eternity. Finally, Hans pocketed the knife and slid down the tree. The boys gripped the end of the rope and walked slowly around the tree, unwinding the wraps as they went. When there were one-and-a-half wraps left, the rope began to slide.

"All right, easy now," Hans said. "Let's take it slow."

By letting the rope slide slowly around the tree, Hans and Philipe lowered the unconscious form carefully to the ground. When the man's boots touched the ground, Hans and Gretchen held the line while Philipe gently guided him to the best possible position.

Hans leaned over the unconscious form on the ground. "Archer," he read aloud. "That must be his name."

Philipe touched his arm. "Hans, we have to get him out of here! If the Nazis find us here, we're all dead!"

Hans looked up into the tree. "That chute is a dead giveaway. I wish we could take it down."

At that moment, Gretchen and the boys heard the crunching of leaves as several men scrambled down the ridge toward them. They looked at each other in panic. The soldiers had found them!

7

HIDEAWAY HUT

The three young people crouched in fear beside the unconscious form of the American pilot as the rustling of leaves told them that the approaching soldiers were almost upon them. Hans thought desperately, searching for a way out. Perhaps he, Gretchen, and Philipe could still make an escape, but Hans was unwilling to leave the American to the mercy of the Nazis.

"Hide beneath that bush," he whispered urgently to Gretchen. "Hurry! If the Nazis take us, you can at least tell Papa what happened."

At that moment, the bushes parted to reveal Papa and two of the villagers. Relief swept over Hans. "Papa!" he exclaimed. "We thought you were the soldiers!"

One of the villagers, a tall, thin man with wire-rimmed glasses and a dark stocking cap, stepped forward and took charge. He knelt beside the unconscious pilot, removed one of his gloves, and felt for a pulse. "He's still alive," he reported to the others. "But we need to get him out of here immediately." He glanced up into the tree. "And we need to get that chute down."

The other villager, a short, muscular man named Michel Marceau, hurried to the tree. "I'll do it, *Monsieur* Blanc." He leaped upward, caught a branch, and began to climb.

Martin Blanc unfastened the pilot's chinstrap, then gently removed his helmet. He handed it to Gretchen. "Keep this with you. We can't leave it here."

"*Oui, Monsieur*," Gretchen answered.

Monsieur Blanc glanced toward Philipe. "Philipe, why don't you help *Monsieur* Marceau get that parachute out of the tree? The rest of us will make a stretcher and get this airman out of here before the Nazis find us."

As Philipe climbed the tree, *Monsieur* Blanc pulled a small hatchet from his belt and used it to quickly chop down two small saplings. Placing the two poles half a meter apart, he then used Philipe's rope to hastily rig a crisscross webbing between them to form a makeshift stretcher. Hans' father helped him carefully lift the pilot onto the stretcher as Hans held the man's injured legs.

"We'll take him to Gambier's old hut," *Monsieur* Blanc called to *Monsieur* Marceau. "Dispose of the chute and then meet us there."

He turned to Hans. "You're a sturdy lad. Think you can carry one corner of the stretcher?"

Hans nodded.

With Papa at the back end of the stretcher, Hans and *Monsieur* Blanc at the front corners, and Gretchen carrying the pilot's helmet, the rescue party began to struggle up the mountainside. They had scarcely gone two hundred meters when they spotted another villager helping with the search, and he took one of the corners from Hans' father. Three minutes later, they had reached an old logging road.

"There's a hermit's hut just over a kilometer from here," *Monsieur* Blanc told the others as they hurried along the rutted road. "We'll take him there."

The unconscious pilot suddenly thrashed his arms and muttered something in English, then said it again in French. "The eagle! Gotta find the eagle!"

Hans looked at Papa. "What's he talking about? What is 'the eagle'?"

Papa shook his head. "I don't know, Son. The man's delirious."

"Papa!" Gretchen shouted, "there's a jeep!"

The road dipped through the bottom of a rocky gully, with the banks on each side rising three or four meters above them. A Nazi jeep with two soldiers aboard had appeared suddenly on the bank to their left. The soldier on the passenger side leaped to his feet and raised his rifle to cover them. "Don't anyone move!" he shouted.

An explosion shattered the stillness of the forest as it lifted one side of the jeep into the air. The vehicle tumbled end over end toward the rescue party below. Papa just managed to leap clear as it thundered past. The two soldiers were thrown from the jeep by the force of the blast, and now lay motionless on the hillside.

"Let's get out of here!" Papa cried. "The explosion may attract other troops!" The rescuers raced down the road.

"Papa," Hans gasped, "what caused the explosion?"

"I have no idea, Son," Papa replied. "It was almost as if a grenade went off!"

Ten minutes later, *Monsieur* Blanc called a halt. "Let's set the stretcher down for a moment," he said. "I'm looking for a trail, and it may take me a few minutes to find it."

The others waited anxiously while he searched the woods. "It's hardly more than a rabbit trail," he told Papa. "You have to be right on top of it before you see it. But I'm sure this is the place. It's around here somewhere."

Finally, he found the path nearly a hundred meters back down the road. The rescuers had walked right past without even seeing it.

"We're only a few hundred meters away from our goal," *Monsieur* Blanc told the others. "But this will be the toughest part of the journey."

He was right. It took them over half an hour to carry, drag, or push the stretcher the last few hundred meters. The trail twisted and climbed through canyons, ravines and gullies. At times, it seemed to disappear completely. But *Monsieur* Blanc knew where he was going and kept the rescuers from losing their way. Twice they used the leftover rope to hoist the stretcher up small precipices.

"Well, here we are," *Monsieur* Blanc said as he set one end of the stretcher on the ground. "This is Gambier's hut."

Hans looked about. There was no sign of any sort of dwelling. But *Monsieur* Blanc stepped over, seized what appeared to be a cluster of dead vines, and pulled. To the amazement of the others, a cleverly disguised door swung open on leather hinges.

Hans stared in astonishment. A small hut had been built right into the side of the mountain, then disguised so completely that it was not visible from three meters away!

He stepped to the doorway and peered inside. The shanty was tiny, perhaps two meters by three, but boasted a bed, a table and chair, and diminutive fireplace. A tiny window admitted a small amount of light.

Hans stepped back outside, searching for the window, and at first had difficulty locating it. The opening had been cleverly camouflaged with a network of dead branches and vines.

"Let's get him inside," *Monsieur* Blanc urged. "*Monsieur* Von Edler, you get one end of the stretcher, and I'll get the other. We'll set the stretcher beside the bed, then lift him into it."

As the two men carried the unconscious pilot inside, Philipe and *Monsieur* Marceau came hurrying up. "How is the American?" *Monsieur* Marceau asked.

Hans shook his head. "He's still unconscious."

Philipe stepped to the door of the hut, looked inside for a moment, then turned to *Monsieur* Marceau. "What is this place?"

"It was built by a hermit named Gambier," the man replied. "We called him 'the rabbit man.' He came into town every three months or so for supplies, for which he traded furs—usually rabbit furs. He lived mostly on small game that he trapped in snares, and he got his water from a nearby spring. *Monsieur* Blanc and I were hunting up here several years ago and stumbled onto this hut by accident. Gambier was outraged that we had found his home. He left a few days later, and no one has ever seen him since. Except for *Monsieur* Blanc and me, no one in Messiere even knows that this place is here."

The group hurried inside the tiny hut. *Monsieur* Marceau pulled off his hat to reveal an unruly shock of flaming red hair. "Let's get a fire going and warm this place up," he said.

"Wait!" Hans protested. "The Nazis will see the smoke!"

Monsieur Marceau chuckled. "I doubt if they will, boy. Gambier vented this little fireplace right into the side of the mountain. Apparently, there's some sort of a cavern beneath the mountainside. *Monsieur* Blanc and I built a roaring fire in this little fireplace last fall, then went out to see if we could find the smoke. After an hour, we found small traces of smoke coming out of the mountainside more than two hundred meters from here! It was the most amazing thing I had ever seen!"

The American stirred, and the little group gathered along the side of the narrow bed. "We need to get Doc Nilsson up here right away," *Monsieur* Marceau said. "This man needs immediate attention!"

"Before we do anything else," *Monsieur* Blanc declared, "it needs to be understood that no one mentions this hut or this pilot to anyone! Not even to family members! The seven of us are the only ones who even know of the existence of this hut. We'll have to bring

Doctor Nilsson into our confidence, and that will make eight. But no one says a word to anyone! Is that understood?"

"*Oui, Monsieur*," several voices uttered.

"Philipe, I know you, and I believe I can trust you to keep this quiet. Am I correct?"

"*Oui, Monsieur*," Philipe answered.

Monsieur Blanc turned to Papa. "I don't know you well, *Monsieur* Von Edler, nor your children. Can these young people be trusted to keep a secret?"

Papa smiled. "*Oui, Monsieur*. They've already been tested in that regard. More than you'll ever know!"

Monsieur Blanc turned to *Monsieur* Marceau. "Go for Doc Nilsson," he said. "Make sure that he understands the need for secrecy and that the location of the hut is not to be revealed to anyone for any reason. I think we can trust him." *Monsieur* Marceau nodded and left immediately.

Monsieur Blanc turned to Papa and the other villager. "I'll stay here with the American. Why don't you take the kids and work over our trail, just to be sure that there are no signs to lead the Nazis to this hut? I'm afraid we left quite a track in the places where we dragged that stretcher. I'll dismantle the stretcher while I wait for the doctor."

The American suddenly opened his eyes. "Where are we?" he asked, in English. Seeing the strange looks that were given him, he asked again, in French. "Where are we?"

"You're with friends," *Monsieur* Blanc assured him, kneeling beside the bed. "You're in a hut three kilometers from the French village of Messiere. The place is well hidden from the Nazis."

The American suddenly groaned and a grimace of anguish crossed his features. "My legs!"

"We're going for a doctor now, *Monsieur*. You'll be well cared for."

The pilot closed his eyes for a moment, and those in the room could see that he was in tremendous pain. He gritted his teeth and took several quick, shallow breaths.

Suddenly he opened his eyes, raised up in the bed, and grabbed *Monsieur* Blanc's hand in a desperate grip. "I must find the silver eagle," he said, his eyes wild with urgent pleading. "You have to help me find the silver eagle!"

His eyes fell closed, and he dropped back upon the bed.

8

MAJOR ARCHER

The next day was Sunday, and the Von Edlers walked to the little church in the village. Five German soldiers stood on the front steps outside the building, but the villagers simply filed past them, and so Papa, Hans, and Gretchen did the same.

The sanctuary was nearly full in spite of the soldiers, and Papa, Hans, and Gretchen took a seat near the back. "Look at the beautiful stained-glass windows, Papa," Gretchen whispered, "and all the carved woodwork, and the white stone altar! This church is wonderful!"

"It is beautiful," Papa agreed in a whisper, "but that's not what makes a church."

The choir filed in, and the worshippers grew quiet. After several numbers by the choir, the minister ascended the pulpit. He was wearing a long, white robe with a wide, black collar that met in the front in the shape of a "V." The hem of his robe and the cuffs of his sleeves were fringed in gold, and a gold sash with fringed ends draped across both sides of his chest. He stepped up into the high pulpit at one side of the sanctuary and began to speak.

After a few minutes, Gretchen leaned over to Papa. "I can't even understand what he's talking about!" she whispered.

Papa sighed. "It really doesn't matter," he whispered. "He's not preaching the Gospel."

As the Von Edlers walked back up the lane after the service, Hans said, "That minister really didn't preach the truth, did he? I noticed that he didn't even open a Bible!"

Papa nodded. "This is not a Gospel-preaching church, Hans. That man was teaching salvation by works, not salvation through faith in the blood of Jesus. We won't go back any more."

"But it's the only church in the village!" Gretchen replied.

Papa nodded sadly. "*Oui*, that it is. But we can't honor the Lord by attending a church that doesn't preach and teach the truth. The apostle Paul told the Corinthians to separate themselves from the worship of unbelievers, and that also applies to us today. We can't go to a church that teaches a false gospel."

"Then what will we do?" Hans asked.

"I suppose we'll have our own service on Sunday morning," Papa replied. "It won't be the same as going to church, but I believe that for us it's the right thing to do."

He put his arms around Hans and Gretchen. "Let's hurry home and see if *Madame* Dubois has dinner ready, shall we? After we eat, I want to hike up to check on the American pilot to see if there's anything we can do."

It took thirty-five minutes to hike to the hut where the injured pilot was hidden. Papa had stressed the need to be on the constant lookout for the German troops, and Hans spotted four grenadieres on the trail in time to slip into the woods without being seen. After hiding in a thicket for five minutes, they continued up to the hideaway without incident.

Monsieur Blanc opened the door of the hut as they approached, and Hans was surprised to see that Philipe was inside. "How's the American?" Papa asked, as they stepped through the tiny doorway.

"Both his legs were broken, as we thought, as well as his collarbone," the villager answered. "Doc Nilsson set and splinted his legs and taped his collarbone. He told us that the broken legs seemed to be simple fractures and should heal well. So that's good news."

"Has he regained consciousness?"

Monsieur Blanc shook his head. "Only briefly, two or three times. He says that he's Major Daniel Archer, but we're not sure if he's even in his right mind. He's begged us several times to find the silver eagle, whatever that is."

"Are you going to move him down to the village or maybe try to get him out of the region?" Papa asked.

The tall villager shook his head again. "Doc Nilsson says he shouldn't be moved any more than necessary. You know what the trail coming up here is like. And if the Nazis caught us taking him down, there would be nothing we could do to keep him out of their hands. We decided he's safest staying right here until he recovers. *Monsieur* Marceau and I are taking turns staying with him, and the doctor has agreed to come every three days to check on him."

Hans knelt beside the bed and studied the American pilot. The man was lean-faced, with a square jaw and rugged, handsome features. For some reason, Hans decided he looked like a man who could be trusted. *So this is an American*, he thought.

The injured pilot abruptly opened his eyes and looked straight at Hans. "Well, hello, lad. Who are you, and where am I?" He was speaking excellent French, with hardly a trace of a foreign accent.

Hans was taken by surprise. "Papa, he's awake!" he blurted.

"Where am I?" the pilot asked again.

Papa knelt beside him. "You are in a small hut outside the village of Messiere, *Monsieur*. You have been injured, and we are hiding you from the Germans."

"My plane was shot down, wasn't it?" the pilot said. "I'm beginning to remember now."

"Do you know what day this is?" *Monsieur* Blanc asked, trying to determine if the American was thinking straight.

"How long have I been here?"

"We brought you here yesterday," *Monsieur* Blanc replied.

The pilot thought for a moment. "Then this is Sunday, November 15, 1942."

Papa and *Monsieur* Blanc looked at each other. "I think he's back!" Papa said.

"This is *Monsieur* Von Edler," the tall villager told the pilot, "and these are his children, Hans and Gretchen. This is Philipe, and I am *Monsieur* Blanc. These young people found you in a tree yesterday, and we brought you to a place where the Nazis won't find you. Our doctor has set your broken legs, and you have had two doses of morphine. And now, who are you?"

The pilot smiled. "It sounds like I have been well cared for, and I am grateful. I'm Major Daniel Archer of the United States Air Force. I was testing a new piece of armament before I was shot down, and it was doing very well! As a matter of fact . . ."

He suddenly paused, and a look of concern crossed his friendly face. "Did you find my bird?"

Monsieur Blanc frowned. "Your bird, Major? I'm afraid we don't understand."

Major Archer laughed, then grunted in pain. "I'm sorry, I should have said my airplane. Did you find my airplane?"

A light suddenly came on for Hans. "Is your airplane the *Silver Eagle*?"

The major grinned. "*Oui*! That's it! Did you find the *Eagle*?"

Monsieur Blanc shook his head. "No, Major, we have not found it. You asked for it a number of times while you were unconscious, but we have seen no sign of the aircraft. Our main concern was to keep you out of the hands of the Nazis."

Major Archer nodded. "I appreciate your concern for me, but we must find my airplane." He fell silent for a moment, and Hans could tell he was deep in thought.

The major looked from one man to the other. "Did anyone see where my plane went down?" he asked. "It's vital that we find it!"

"I'm sure it's badly damaged, Major," *Monsieur* Blanc said. "There's no way you could ever fly it out . . ."

The pilot laughed. "I wasn't hoping for that much, *Monsieur*. But it's important that we find that plane! We have to!"

"Why is the plane so important?" Hans asked.

Major Archer thoughtfully looked from one face to another. It was obvious he was struggling with a decision. Finally, he spoke. "I'll have to take you into my confidence," he said. "My life's in your hands, anyway."

He paused, grimacing in pain, and the others leaned forward eagerly. "I guess you know that the Luftwaffe has had air superiority over the Allies for some time now," he said. "Hitler's little Focke-Wulfs and Messerschmitts can fly circles around most of the birds we're flying!"

Major Archer coughed, then asked for a glass of water. *Monsieur* Blanc poured him a tin cup full, which he drank gratefully. *"Merci, Monsieur."*

"Anyway, as I was saying, the Jerries can out-fly almost anything we have in the air. The Messerschmitts have a top speed of four hundred twenty-some miles per hour. That's well over six hundred fifty kilometers per hour. The only thing that even comes close is the British Hawker Typhoon."

The pilot coughed a couple of times and then continued. "Well anyway, some of us have decided that if we can't out-fly the Nazis, then we have to outshoot them. Two weapons-specialist friends and I have developed a rapid-fire cannon that will outshoot the British Vickers gun or the old American standby, the Lewis gun.

"As you know, a cannon fires a heavier, faster shell than the machine gun does, and the shell is explosive, rather than solid. But the pilots have a hard time shooting as accurately as they can with a machine gun. We think we've developed the best of both—a cannon that is as easy to fire accurately as the machine gun, but packs a far greater punch! And it fires incredibly fast, clipping out half again as many rounds as any previous cannon!"

Major Archer grimaced in pain, but then continued. "The cannon is code-named the 'Joe Louis' after the American heavyweight boxing champion because they both pack quite a punch." He grinned. "If we could mount the Joe Louis on every Allied aircraft, Hitler wouldn't know what hit him!"

Monsieur Blanc interrupted. "So tell us, Major, why is it so important to find your plane?"

"We have reason to believe the Nazis knew we were working on the Joe Louis," the major replied. "There were two different attempts to steal it before we even got it mounted on an aircraft. If the Germans find out that my prototype is lying up here somewhere on this mountain, they'll move heaven and earth to get to it. The Allies have to finish developing that gun and get it into production before the Germans do! If this cannon proves to be what we think it is, one month with the Joe Louis could make the difference in air superiority."

"So you were field-testing the Joe Louis yesterday when you were shot down," Papa said.

Archer nodded. "With my rank and my access to classified secrets, I'm no longer even supposed to be in an aircraft in combat. But I wanted to see for myself what the

Joe Louis would do in combat, and I wasn't going to put any of my men into combat with an untested weapon."

"We saw you in the dogfight against the Messerschmitts," Philipe told the major. "So that's why you did so well against them! We saw you take out four planes!"

"Four kills in one encounter is a fantastic record for any flier," the pilot agreed. "You can imagine what could happen if every Allied flier had a weapon like this! That's why we have to find that plane before the Nazis do!"

9

THE SEARCH

The following day dawned clear and cold. The wind gusted and howled outside the windows of the little farmhouse as the family sat down to breakfast. "*Monsieur* Blanc stopped by a few minutes ago," *Monsieur* Dubois told Papa as he passed steaming bowls of corn meal mush. "He said that he needs you to help him with an emergency project for the next couple of days."

"What about the barn?" Papa asked.

"Go help *Monsieur* Blanc," the farmer replied. "We'll get back to the barn later. I'm not feeling too well today, anyhow. This will give me an excuse to stay inside where it's warm."

He spooned a tiny bit of sugar into a steaming mug of tea. "*Monsieur* Blanc wants you to meet him at his barn at eight o'clock."

"May we go too, Papa?" Hans asked.

Papa nodded. "If he doesn't want you there, he'll say so."

Hans and Gretchen followed Papa into *Monsieur* Blanc's barn to find fifteen men from the village waiting inside. "I believe we're all here, now," *Monsieur* Blanc said, as they stepped through the door. "Let's get started right away."

The men grew quiet.

"As many of you know," the tall villager said, speaking loudly enough for all to hear, "an American plane was shot down over Messiere Saturday afternoon. The pilot survived and was taken to a place of safety. I'll not go into details. I'll ask those of you who know about it to remain tight-lipped, and I'll ask those of you who don't know to refrain from asking."

He looked from one man to another until he had made eye contact with every one. "I called you here today because I believe that each of you can be trusted. What we do today is not to be discussed with anyone outside this barn, including your wives. I will say this—if we are successful today, we may have a part in bringing this horrendous war to a speedier conclusion."

Monsieur Blanc's gaze swept over the group again. "Now, do each of you understand the need for secrecy, and pledge to keep this matter under your hat?" He waited until each man had nodded, then continued.

"The American was flying a Lockheed P-38 Lightning. It went down on the east slope of Mount Piedler, probably above the old logging road that runs south from the camp. I won't go into details, but it is imperative that we find this plane. I see that many of you brought ropes and climbing gear, as I requested. Good. We'll regroup in just a few minutes at the old quarry below the mining camp, then walk a sweep south. If we don't find the plane by one o'clock, two of the ladies of the village will provide us with a hot meal. Are there any questions?"

"What does the plane look like?" one man called.

"Right now I'm afraid it looks rather crumpled and bent," *Monsieur* Blanc replied, and the men laughed.

"Excuse my levity at a time like this," Blanc said. "The plane is aluminum skinned, unpainted, so it appears silver in color. It's a twin boom design, which means that it has two fuselages. You'll recognize the USA star emblem."

Most of the men nodded.

"Why are those kids here?" another man asked.

"Those kids are Hans and Gretchen Von Edler. They and their father are newcomers to the village, but they've already proven themselves trustworthy to my satisfaction."

The questioner shrugged.

"One more thing before we go," the tall leader said.

The men grew quiet again.

"The Nazis are aware that this plane went down and, for some reason, are as eager as we are to find it. You may encounter them on the mountainside, so be prepared to evade any questions they may ask, and realize that you are at risk. If possible, just try to avoid being seen."

He opened the barn door. "Gentlemen, we must find the aircraft before the Germans do. If we are successful, we may be able to send them home to Germany, and that would mean a tremendous saving of life. Let's slip out by twos and threes to avoid attracting attention. We'll meet by the quarry in fifteen minutes."

As the men slipped out in small groups into the cold, Hans noticed that *Monsieur* Marceau was not present, and concluded that he was at the hut with Major Archer.

The searchers huddled together at the entrance to the rock quarry. The wind howled, scattering the autumn leaves and making the cold temperatures even more unbearable. Dark clouds obscured the top of the mountain, creating an ominous atmosphere.

"Where's Philipe?" Hans whispered, as *Monsieur* Blanc came striding up to the group.

"He's with *Messieurs* Marceau and Archer," *Monsieur* Blanc replied quietly. "He's serving as a courier and errand boy."

He raised his voice and addressed the shivering group. "We'll spread out in a line, each man twenty meters from the next," he instructed. "We'll sweep south till we reach the southern point of Mount Piedler, then regroup and make another sweep north. We'll be covering some rough terrain, but try to stay within hailing distance of the next person in line. Be alert, and watch out for Nazi troops. Good luck, and God bless!"

Gretchen was assigned to walk the logging road, with Hans as the second in line twenty meters above her. She shivered as she walked along, her gaze sweeping both sides of the road. She had walked only a few hundred meters when she was startled to see a figure walking toward her. Gretchen debated stepping into the woods to avoid being seen, but the person on the road was obviously not a soldier, so she decided against it.

As the stranger approached, Gretchen was surprised to recognize Colette Duval. "Hello, Colette," she said hesitantly.

"What are you doing here?" Colette demanded.

"I'm sorry, Colette, but I really can't tell you," Gretchen answered.

"Where's Philipe?"

"I-I don't know. I haven't seen him today."

"You'd better tell me," the taller girl demanded, stepping closer to Gretchen.

"I-I don't know," Gretchen repeated.

"You're hiding something—I can tell. Now, where is my brother?"

"I don't know!" Gretchen said emphatically. "I haven't seen him since Saturday!"

"Then he was with you and your brother Saturday, wasn't he? What were you doing up here?"

"I can't tell you!" Gretchen insisted.

"Why not?"

"I just can't!"

"Well, you're gonna tell me, and you're gonna tell me now!" Colette grabbed both ends of Gretchen's scarf and twisted them together, creating pressure against Gretchen's throat. "Now tell me—why are you up here?"

"I can't tell you!" Gretchen wailed. "Please stop! You're hurting me!"

"Tell me!" The scarf twisted tighter.

"Colette, you're choking me!" Gretchen sobbed. The scarf was twisted so tightly that she dropped to her knees. But she dared not tell what she knew, for Colette would surely go right to the Nazis.

"I'm not gonna let you up until you tell me," Colette snarled savagely. She twisted the scarf tighter still.

Gretchen was desperate. She pulled at the scarf, trying frantically to get her fingers inside the loop around her throat. But the thick fabric was twisted far too tight for that. *Lord, help me!* she prayed silently, helplessly. Her vision blurred, and she realized that she was about to black out.

10

THE SEARCH CONTINUES

Gretchen tried desperately to free herself, but the bigger girl continued to twist the scarf relentlessly. *Lord Jesus, help me!* Gretchen prayed.

In spite of her distress, Gretchen heard Colette grunt in pain, and the force of the scarf suddenly lessened. Gretchen pulled the twisted scarf open and gratefully gulped the frigid air. She looked up through her tears to see Hans standing beside her with his fists raised.

"You hit me!" Colette screamed.

"And I'll slug you again if you don't leave my sister alone," Hans vowed.

"You hit me!" Colette was nearly hysterical. "Don't you know you're not supposed to hit a girl?"

Hans snorted in disgust. "It doesn't matter," he answered evenly. "You're a bully! And I'll hit any bully that hurts my sister!"

Colette darted down the road and then twisted around to face them. "I'm gonna tell Philipe!" she threatened.

"I'm sure that Philipe will understand," Hans replied.

Hans helped Gretchen to her feet, then stood with his hand on her shoulder as they watched the other girl race angrily down the road. "Thank you, Hans," Gretchen sobbed. "She tried to make me tell her what we were looking for. I thought she was gonna kill me!"

Hans was angry. "I tried to control my temper, but it was about all I could do to keep from flattening her!" He shook his head. "Are you all right?"

Gretchen tried to stifle a sob. "I think so."

Hans squeezed her shoulder. "Did you tell her anything?"

Gretchen looked up at him. "Oh, no, Hans! I didn't dare tell her anything! She'd just go right to the Nazis!"

Hans smiled. "I'm proud of you, Gretchen." He let out a long sigh. "If she ever tries that again, I'll do more than just punch her once!"

He looked up the road. "We'd better hurry and catch up with the others!"

The search party worked its way down to the southern end of Mount Piedler without finding any trace of the missing airplane. They moved the line farther up the ridge and worked north, but again without success. When they had completed a second pass to the south and returned without success, *Monsieur* Blanc called a break.

"Let's head down to *Madame* Marceau's house," he told his tired, cold volunteers. "She and *Madame* Sanvoisin have hot *cassoulet*, fresh bread, and hot cider waiting for us. It will be good to eat and warm up, *oui*?"

The search party slipped down the hill by twos and threes to gather at the Marceau's farm at the foot of the mountain. Hans and Gretchen walked down with *Monsieur* Brisard, the Messiere banker.

Monsieur Brisard was a small, thin man. As he took off his gloves to blow his nose, Hans saw the soft, white hands of a man unaccustomed to hard physical labor.

"Hey!" Hans said after they had hiked for three or four minutes, "we're not going the right way!"

"We'll take a shorter route," the banker told him. "It's a bit quicker, and it will mean fewer people on the main trail for the Nazis to notice."

Moments later the narrow trail led across the face of a sheer rock precipice. Hans and Gretchen hugged the wall, afraid of falling. "Just relax and stay close to the cliff," their guide instructed. "You'll be fine!"

Hans grabbed a root and stepped closer to the edge. The canyon floor was more than a hundred fifty meters below. He kicked a small rock into space and watched it fall and fall and fall. He let out his breath in a long sigh as he backed away from the edge.

The trail angled sharply downward as it curved its way back into the woods. Hans and Gretchen breathed a sigh of relief. But their gratitude was short-lived: the trail wound its way to the very edge of the canyon again.

Monsieur Brisard noticed their discomfort. "Just a little farther," he encouraged. "Then the trail cuts back into the woods, if you're more comfortable with that. But the canyon trail is the quickest route."

"I'm fine here," Hans declared, ashamed to admit that he was scared and expecting that Gretchen would insist on taking the safer route.

But to his surprise, Gretchen also put up a fearless front. "If Hans can handle it, so can I," she announced.

Moments later, they passed beneath a rusty cable extending across the canyon. Hans pointed to it. "What's that for?"

"The mining camp is just beyond us over that rise," *Monsieur* Brisard explained. "That cable runs across the canyon, crosses the village, and lands at the foot of Mount Andriese on the other side. When the mining camp was in operation, the cable was used to send orders and tools to the shop below, which was much faster than carrying them down by vehicle. On occasion, certain miners have demonstrated their courage by riding a heavy-duty pulley equipped with hand brakes."

"Not me!" Hans declared, gripping a sizeable boulder as his eyes followed the cable down. "That would be one fast terrifying ride!"

The banker grinned. "But you have to admit, it's the fastest way down!"

Ten minutes later, they reached *Monsieur* Marceau's farm several minutes ahead of the rest of the search party. They hurried inside to rest and warm up.

"I've been thinking about Colette," Hans said as he removed his gloves and warmed his hands before the blazing fireplace.

"Well, don't!" Gretchen replied. "The less we think of her, the better!"

Hans nodded. "I know how you feel, Gretchen. But I've been thinking. She needs the Lord, you know!"

Gretchen shrugged. "So she does. But she wouldn't listen even if someone tried to talk to her about it."

"I think you ought to try to witness to her."

Gretchen was shocked. "Hans!" she retorted. "Did you see what she did to me? She almost killed me! She probably would have if you hadn't stopped her!"

"But she needs the Lord," Hans insisted. "Someone needs to try to reach her. She'll die and go to hell if she doesn't get saved."

Gretchen turned toward the fire and rubbed her hands together. "Right now, the idea of Colette Duval going to hell doesn't bother me a whole lot."

"Gretchen!" Hans scolded. "How can you say that?"

His sister shrugged. "Colette doesn't deserve to go to heaven."

"None of us do," Hans replied. "But for the grace of God, we'd all be going to hell! But Colette needs to be saved, and someone needs to witness to her."

"Then why don't you do it?"

"I will if I get a chance," Hans replied seriously, "but it would be better if you did it, since you're a girl."

"All right, if you're so concerned, have you witnessed to Philipe?"

"Not yet. But I'm praying for an opportunity. I'm going to talk to him about the Lord the first chance I get. But I think you ought to be willing to witness to Colette."

"I'm not sure I even want to, Hans," Gretchen said. "If I don't talk to her, someone else will. We're not the only Christians in the whole world, you know."

The door opened just then, and several villagers hurried inside, stomping feet and clapping hands to restore circulation to cold fingers and toes. They rushed to the fireplace to warm up, ending any opportunity for further discussion.

When the last of the search party had come in, *Madame* Marceau called the hungry group into the kitchen. "Come and get something to eat," she urged. "There's hot *cassoulet*, hot cider, and fresh bread! After you have been out in the cold so long, a hot meal will feel mighty good!"

"Let's thank God for safety in our search so far," Papa suggested as he, Hans, and Gretchen sat down with dishes of hot food, "and thank Him for the hot meal we are about to eat. Hans, would you lead us?"

Hans looked about the room. Apparently no one else was planning to pray before they ate: they had all started right in on their meal. Hans felt uncomfortable as he bowed his head.

"Father in heaven," Hans prayed, "we thank you for your provision at the hands of *Madame* Marceau and *Madame* Sanvoisin. Thank you for providing a hot meal for our weary bodies. We are grateful for safety in our search, and we ask for guidance and strength this afternoon. Lead us, Lord, to the American's plane before the Germans find it. We pray in Jesus' name. Amen."

As the hungry group was enjoying the hot meal, *Monsieur* Blanc slipped over to stand beside Hans. "Stay around after the others head for the mountain again," he whispered. "I'll have you take food to Major Archer."

Hans nodded. "But what about Gretchen?"

"She can go with you," the man replied. "You two can stay with Major Archer, and Philipe and *Monsieur* Marceau can take your place in the search line."

Hans nodded again. *"Merci."*

"We'll meet in twenty minutes at the entrance to the mining camp," *Monsieur* Blanc announced when nearly everyone had finished eating. "Slip out in small groups, and try to take various routes to the camp. We should be able to make six more passes across the mountain before dark, but, hopefully, we'll find the plane before then."

Hans and Gretchen lingered behind as the others slipped out into the cold in small groups. When everyone else had gone, *Madame* Marceau handed Hans a small, green duffel bag. "There's a kettle of *cassoulet* in here," she told him, "So try to keep it upright. I wrapped it in some cloth, so I think it will stay warm until you get there. Be careful!"

The wind howled as they stepped into the woods and hurried up the narrow trail. Gusts of wind rattled the branches of trees and spun autumn leaves in circles about their heads. Gretchen wrapped her scarf tighter about her face. "It sure is cold!"

Hans nodded in agreement. "This wind isn't helping. I'm rather glad we can stay with Major Archer instead of staying out in the cold to help with the search."

They were nearly halfway up the mountainside when Gretchen suddenly stopped. "Hans, someone's coming!"

Hans quickly knelt and thrust the duffel bag beneath a small bush and then did his best to cover it with leaves. As Hans stood to his feet, Klause lumbered into view with an enormous load of wood upon his back.

"*G-guten tag*, Klause," Gretchen faltered, but the deaf woodcutter stumbled past as if he had not even seen them standing in the trail. Ten meters past them, he twisted around and stared at them for a few seconds, then turned and continued on down the trail.

Hans shook his head. "I feel sorry for that poor man." He knelt to retrieve the food from under the bush.

Gretchen nodded as she watched Klause disappear around a bend in the trail. "I still don't see how Colette can be so hateful to Klause," she replied. "She ought to be thankful that she's not deaf."

Fifteen minutes later they reached the hideaway hut where the injured American was hidden. Hans opened the camouflaged door, and *Monsieur* Marceau leaped to his feet in alarm. "Oh, it's you," he said in relief as he sank back down on a small stool. "You gave us quite a scare!"

Philipe stepped over and carefully closed the door behind Gretchen.

"We brought dinner," Hans announced as he set the duffel bag on the floor. "How is Major Archer?"

"Major Archer is making it just fine, thank you," a voice from the bed announced, and Hans and Gretchen turned toward the sound. The injured pilot weakly lifted his hand and managed a thin smile. Two days' growth of beard darkened the lower part of his face, giving him a fierce, unfriendly appearance.

Hans stepped to the bed. "We're searching for the *Silver Eagle*," he announced. "We've already made four passes across the mountain, and *Monsieur* Blanc figures we can make six more before nightfall."

Major Archer nodded. "I'm grateful. I just hope we can find it before the Jerries do."

Gretchen opened the duffel bag. "We brought hot food for everyone," she declared. "There's hot *cassoulet* and cider, and *Madame* Marceau's fresh bread! It's a good dinner."

Hans helped *Monsieur* Marceau prop the pilot's shoulders up in the bed, then he and Gretchen watched as the other three devoured the delicious meal. "These French women are outstanding cooks," Major Archer commented as he finished. "Please tell your wife, *Monsieur* Marceau, that the meal was excellent!"

Hans turned to *Monsieur* Marceau. "*Monsieur* Blanc wants Gretchen and me to stay with the Major for a while," he said. "He wants you and Philipe to join in the search for the plane."

The villager nodded. "Where are they working?"

"They should be making a sweep along the top of the first ridge," Hans answered. "They start parallel to the mining camp and work south."

"They shouldn't be too hard to find," the man said. "Are the Nazis searching?"

Hans nodded. "They're all over the mountain! Be careful!"

Philipe and *Monsieur* Marceau bundled up against the cold and then slipped from the tiny hut. Hans carefully closed the door behind them.

"So, *Mademoiselle,* what's your name?" Major Archer asked Gretchen.

"Gretchen Von Edler."

"This your brother? He looks a lot like you."

Gretchen nodded. "His name is Hans. We're new here. We came from Switzerland."

"Von Edler," the pilot repeated. "That's German, isn't it?"

Hans knelt beside the narrow bed. "We're really from Austria," he said, "but we had to leave. We'll get to go back to Austria after the war is over."

The pilot grinned. "Couldn't take *Anschluss*, huh? I can't say that I blame you."

Hans shook his head. "It was more than that." He hesitated, and Major Archer noticed.

"You know my secret, Hans. But there's no need to tell me yours, unless you want to."

Hans thought for a moment. "All right," he said finally. "But promise me you won't share this with anyone?"

The American pilot nodded. "I promise."

"Gretchen and I helped a Jewish boy escape Austria to get away from the *Gestapo*," he began. "Jacob was the son of a double agent for the Allies. We didn't know it at first, but he was carrying some top-secret papers for his father.

Before it was all over, I think half of Hitler's SS forces were chasing us!"

Hans watched Major Archer's face as he told the rest of the story, and he could see that the man was impressed by the tale. "So that's why we left Austria," Hans finished.

The pilot laughed. "So we're all three fugitives from the Nazis, eh? I make you a deal—you don't lead them to me, and I won't tell them where to find you!"

Hans laughed. "Deal!"

Major Archer turned to Gretchen. "So you're an Allied agent, huh? I never would have guessed it. Those agents are getting prettier and prettier!"

Gretchen smiled shyly, embarrassed at the attention the major was paying her.

"Hans," the major said, "get me a cup of water, would you? My throat's a bit parched from all this talking."

Hans filled the tin cup from the bucket beside the table and handed it to the pilot. "So what will happen if we can't find your plane?" he asked. "I mean, if the Nazis find it first?"

The major took a drink of water. "Thanks, pal." He emptied the cup, then handed it back to Hans.

"We think the Nazis know that we were developing the Joe Louis," the major replied. "Remember, there were two separate attempts to steal it. If they recover the Joe Louis from my plane and develop it before the Allies do, it will increase German air superiority that much more. But if the Allies develop it first, we may be able to claim superiority in the air. That would go a long way toward winning the war."

"But if we have it first and one of our planes gets shot down, couldn't the Germans copy it?"

"Sure," the pilot replied. "But time would be on our side. Just one month with the Joe Louis could make a tremendous difference as to which side has the advantage in the air. That's why we have to find the *Eagle* before the Nazis do!"

Gretchen touched Hans on the arm. "I don't feel good, Hans. I want to go home."

Hans frowned. "We can't go now, Gretchen. Someone has to stay here with the major. We have to wait till *Monsieur* Blanc or Marceau come back."

"I can go back by myself," Gretchen told him, "and you can stay here."

"What if you run into the soldiers?" Hans asked. "They're all over this mountain!"

"I'll take the canyon trail down," Gretchen replied. "It's faster and shorter. And I'd have less chance of running into the Nazis."

Hans shrugged. "All right, but be careful."

ଓ ☉ ଛ

Gretchen hurried down the narrow mountain trail. The wind seemed determined to snatch her from the path and hurl her into the canyon, but she pushed on with determination. She slowed down as the trail wound its way to the very brink of the canyon, then crossed a narrow, rocky ledge. Her breath came in short little gasps as she inched her way across. It hadn't seemed this difficult or scary when she was with Hans and *Monsieur* Brisard.

She glanced forward, and her heart skipped a beat. Colette Duval was blocking the trail!

"Where are you going in such a hurry?" Colette mocked, striding forward to seize Gretchen by the sleeve. "Your brother isn't here to help you this time, Precious!"

"Colette, please," Gretchen said. "I'm not feeling well."

The taller girl laughed. "Not feeling well? Then perhaps you should be at home instead of here on the side of this windy mountain!"

"That's where I'm going," Gretchen replied. "Now, let me by, please."

"'Let me by, please,'" Colette mocked. "Not so fast, Precious. This is a good time for you and me to have a little talk."

Gretchen glanced nervously toward the edge of the precipice and scooted closer to the safe side of the trail. Colette noticed. "You're not afraid of heights, are you?"

Gretchen shook her head. "Not much."

"I'm not afraid at all," Colette boasted. "Papa says—" she stopped and swallowed hard, "Papa said that I have the courage of a mountain goat. I'm not afraid of heights."

Colette released her hold on Gretchen's sleeve and grabbed the collar of Gretchen's coat. "Let's see how close you can get to the edge."

Gretchen's heart pounded with fear. "Colette, please," she begged.

Colette laughed as she slowly pulled Gretchen toward the edge of the precipice. Gretchen tried to resist, but the taller girl was much stronger than she was. "You're not afraid, are you, Precious?" Colette taunted.

Fear tightened around Gretchen's heart as Colette, gripping a boulder with one hand, extended her other hand to hold Gretchen's upper body over the side of the cliff. "Colette, don't," she sobbed. "It's more than a hundred meters to the bottom!" She felt dizzy with terror, and she found that she couldn't even breathe.

"You know, Precious, this would be a good time for you to tell me what you and your brother were doing up here on the mountain."

Gretchen shook her head, and her tormentor pushed her slightly farther over the edge. "Tell me!" Colette demanded. "Your brother isn't here to save you!"

Gretchen struggled to draw a breath. "I-I can't," she faltered. "Colette, please. I j-just can't tell you!"

"Tell me, and I'll let you go," Colette promised. She pushed a little harder.

At that moment, the boulder pulled free from the side of the mountain, and Colette lost her grip. She dropped to her knees on the trail, releasing her hold on Gretchen.

With a scream of terror, Gretchen fell over the edge.

11

THE SECRET AGENT

Gretchen's scream echoed across the chasm as she fell over the edge of the precipice. She grabbed in desperation for Colette, but her fingers clutched empty air. As she fell, her shoulder slammed against the sharp edge of the cliff, sending her tumbling. Terror gave way to sudden darkness.

Her mind slowly cleared, and she awoke to find herself lying on her side. Her head throbbed with pain. As she attempted to rise to a sitting position, everything went black again.

Gretchen slowly regained consciousness a second time. She took a deep breath. The pain in her head was sharper now, and she became aware that her back was badly scraped. She tried to roll over further on her side, but for some reason, she couldn't seem to move.

She glanced to her right, and caught her breath. The empty space beneath her told her that she was suspended high on the wall of the canyon! Suddenly, she remembered. She had fallen. She remembered seeing the look of panic on Colette's face. Then it all came back. She had fallen over the edge from the canyon trail!

Her heart pounding with fear, Gretchen slowly reached behind her. Her coat was pulled up behind her, exposing her back to the rough rock wall. She tried to pull free but, through the fog of her confusion, realized that her coat was caught on a rocky projection. So that was why she had not fallen all the way to her death on the canyon floor: as she struck the ledge, her coat had caught on the protruding spur of rock.

Gretchen took a deep breath, then slowly, carefully turned her head to look above her. To her amazement, the edge of the bluff was just a short distance from where she lay. *I only fell three or four meters*, she realized.

She drew another breath. "Colette!" she called. "Help me! I can't move!"

There was no answer.

Gretchen tried again. "Colette! Help me! I can't get back up! Help me!"

A helpless sensation overwhelmed Gretchen as her mind cleared and the danger of her precarious situation sank in. Apparently Colette had fled the scene and would tell no one of Gretchen's plight, especially since she had caused the fall. No one else knew where Gretchen was, or even that she was in trouble, for that matter. If the rock projection behind her gave way, she would tumble the rest of the way to her death.

"Help me, Lord Jesus!" she prayed. "You're the only one who knows where I am! Please send someone down the trail to help me!"

"Help!" she called again. "Help! Somebody help me!"

A sudden fear gripped her. What if the Nazi soldiers heard her?

She decided that it really didn't matter. Anything would be better than falling to her death. Taking a deep breath, she called again. "Help me! Somebody help! HELP!"

Gretchen stopped and caught her breath in sobbing little gasps. She tried to still her rising fear and quiet the frantic pounding of her heart. Her head ached, and the pain in her back intensified. The rocky surface was cold against her bare legs and back, and she reached back to find that her dress was badly ripped. Not that it mattered at a time like this.

"Help!" she called again. "Somebody, please help me!"

The wind gusted and moaned, stinging Gretchen's face with tiny bits of sand. She suddenly felt very cold. *If nobody comes, I'll freeze to death. What if it snows, and they don't find me till next spring? What will Papa think? What will Hans do? What if the searchers start looking for me instead of hunting for Major Archer's airplane?*

Gretchen lay still for a moment, thinking and praying. Hans was the only one who knew that she had taken the canyon trail, or even that she had left the hut. There would be no reason for him to leave the hut until *Monsieur* Marceau or *Monsieur* Blanc came to relieve him. That could be hours from now. And what if Hans took a different trail down?

"Help! Somebody help me! Please, HELP ME!"

"Lord Jesus, don't let me die here without seeing Hans and Papa again!" Gretchen sobbed. She lay quietly for several minutes, trying to think of some way out of her desperate situation.

A tiny pebble struck the side of her face, causing her to jump with fright. As she looked upward, she heard a man cough.

"Help! Somebody, help me!"

"Gretchen?" It was Papa's voice! "Where are you, Sweetheart?"

Relief flooded over Gretchen. "Right below you, Papa! I fell into the canyon!"

More pebbles fell on Gretchen, and then Papa's face appeared above the edge of the precipice. "Oh, my!" he exclaimed in alarm. "Gretchen!"

"I'm all right, Papa!" she tried to reassure him. "But my coat's caught, and I can't move."

"Hold still, Sweetheart!" Papa called frantically. "I have a rope!"

"No, Papa," Gretchen replied. "We won't be able to climb back up without help."

"Gretchen, hold still," Papa insisted. Moments later, a rope tied in several loops came snaking down beside her. "Pass your arms through the loops and hang on," Papa instructed. "I'll tie the other end to a sturdy tree, then go for help."

Gretchen did as she was told.

"I'll be back in less than ten minutes," Papa called. "I love you, Gretchen!"

"I love you, Papa," Gretchen called back. "Please hurry. I'm very cold."

When Papa was gone, a tremendous loneliness gripped her, but it was reassuring to be able to cling to the rope. And Papa had said he would be right back.

After what seemed like an eternity, she heard voices on the trail above. "Hold on, Gretchen!" Papa called. "We'll have you up in no time!"

Moments later, Papa was right beside her, suspended by a thick rope. She turned and grabbed him. "Be calm," he told her. "Don't move until I get this rope around you."

Papa pulled himself up to the ledge, planted one knee on the ledge between Gretchen's knees, then leaned over her and passed a rope behind her back and underneath her arms. When he had tied her securely to himself, he freed her coat. "Thank God this rock held," he whispered.

Gretchen hugged him with all her strength.

"Bring us up!" Papa shouted upwards.

The rope tightened, and Gretchen and her father swung into space, then started upward. Moments later, they were safely on the trail beside the three rescuers. Gretchen threw her arms around her father. "Oh, Papa!" she sobbed, "I want to go home!"

After Papa had thanked the three villagers, he and Gretchen started down the trail for home. "What happened?" Papa asked. "How did you fall from the trail?"

"It was Colette Duval!" Gretchen blurted. "Oh, Papa, I thought she was going to kill me! She tried to scare me into telling what we were doing up here by holding me over the edge. She lost her hold, and I fell!"

Papa's face grew dark with anger. "As soon as I get you home safely, I'll head over and have a talk with *Madame* Duval," he promised.

Gretchen burst into tears. "Oh, Papa," she sobbed, throwing her arms around him, "I'm thankful you came in time!"

Hans and Major Archer looked up as *Monsieur* Marceau, *Monsieur* Blanc, and Philipe Duvall came hurrying into the hut. "There's not a sign of your plane," *Monsieur* Blanc reported to the American pilot. "We've done a quick search of the entire eastern side of the mountain, but nobody found a thing! No plane, no trees sheered off, nothing! That plane went down without leaving a trace!"

Major Archer frowned. "I don't understand that," he replied. "Even if the *Eagle* had exploded and burned, you would still be able to find signs of the crash."

The door opened just then, and Hans' father stepped in. He hurried over to Hans. "Your sister nearly lost her life a short while ago," he said quietly.

"Papa, what happened?" Hans asked in alarm.

"She fell over the edge from the canyon trail," Papa replied. "Thank God, she hit a ledge and her jacket caught on a rock formation. I rappelled down to her and brought her up with the help of some of the men."

"How bad was she hurt?" Hans asked.

Papa shook his head. "Not badly. She scraped her back and banged her head, but I think she'll be fine in a day or two."

Hans frowned. "What made her fall? She seemed like she could handle that trail better than I could."

Papa sighed, trying to hold his emotions in check. "Apparently, she was pushed," he said, "by a girl named Colette."

Hans leaped angrily to his feet. "Colette Duval! She tried to . . ."

Papa held up one hand. "Hopefully, it's taken care of. I had a long talk with *Madame* Duval, and Colette will not be allowed outside for a month! Her mother was very upset, and she apologized over and over again. Apparently, she's having a hard time controlling the girl lately."

Monsieur Marceau snorted. "That's an understatement!"

Philipe bowed his head in shame. "I'm sorry, Hans," he whispered hoarsely.

Hans nodded, acknowledging the apology.

Papa turned his attention to the men in the little room. "I'm sorry to interrupt," he said. "To be honest with you, I didn't even notice anyone but Hans." He stroked his moustache. "Did we find the plane?"

Monsieur Blanc shook his head. "Not a sign of it! That's what we were just discussing. We covered just about all of the eastern slopes and couldn't find a trace of it! It's rather perplexing."

Hans spoke up. "Could the plane possibly have cleared the top of the mountain and crashed on the other side?"

The men looked at Major Archer. "We ruled that out earlier," *Monsieur* Blanc said. "But what do you think? Is there a chance it did?"

The pilot ran a hand over his unshaven jaw. "I don't think so, but I guess we should consider it as a possibility. How high is this mountain?"

Monsieur Marceau spoke up. "I saw a regional map that listed the height as being just over sixteen hundred meters. That's from sea level. The village is right at two hundred meters above sea level."

"Sixteen hundred meters," Archer echoed. "Ninety-six hundred feet." He shook his head. "Then there's no way the *Eagle* cleared the mountain when she went down. I was just above eight thousand feet when I was hit. I bailed out at six thousand."

"So why can't we find her?" Blanc asked, adjusting his glasses. "We didn't walk every square meter of this side of the mountain, of course, but something that size would be hard to miss!"

The pilot shook his head. "It doesn't make sense."

"What if one of the men spotted the plane but didn't report it?" Hans suggested.

Blanc looked at him. "What do you mean, Son?"

"Well, suppose one or two of the men saw the plane, but kept it quiet so they could tell the Nazis? You know, maybe collect a reward, or something?"

Monsieur Blanc shook his head. "Not a chance," he replied emphatically. "I hand-picked all fifteen men. I would trust any of them with my life."

"Well, we'll regroup tomorrow and search the mountain again," *Monsieur* Marceau said. "If the plane went down, it has to . . ."

His words were interrupted by a loud thud from outside the tiny hut. *Monsieur* Blanc leaped to the door and flung it open, then stepped outside. "Come look at this!" he called.

Hans followed the men outside. A piece of brown paper wrapped around a large rock lay beside the door. *Monsieur* Blanc glanced around, then stooped and with a trembling hand picked up the missile. "Someone has found the hut!" he whispered.

Monsieur Blanc unfolded the paper. A puzzled frown creased his face as he scanned the message. "It's written in English," he told the others. "I can read a little, but I don't understand what this says."

"Let's show it to the American," Papa suggested.

Monsieur Blanc nodded. "*Oui*. Of course."

He carried the note inside. The others followed him in.

"*Monsieur* Archer, this message was wrapped around a rock and thrown against the door of the hut," *Monsieur* Blanc began.

The pilot reacted in alarm. "Then they've found the hut!"

Blanc nodded. "*Oui*, someone has. But take a look at this!" He handed the paper to the pilot.

Major Archer glanced at the note. His eyes widened in disbelief, and his hand began to tremble.

12

THE EAGLE

The little group of searchers crowded close to the narrow bed on which the injured pilot lay. A tense silence reigned in the little hut as Major Archer silently read the strange message. His hand trembled, and the color drained from his face.

"Major, what's wrong?" *Monsieur* Marceau asked.

"This is incredible!" the pilot replied. "Absolutely incredible!" He read the note again, then looked up at the others.

"This is from either a personal acquaintance or from someone who knows a lot about me." He coughed nervously, then glanced again at the paper in his hand. "It's written in English, but I'll translate as best I can."

He cleared his throat and looked up again. "This is addressed to 'Archie'! *Messieurs,* 'Archie' was my nickname when I was in high school—what you'd call secondary school, I suppose. As I said, this note was written by someone who knows me, or knows all about me!"

"Read it to us," Hans begged.

Major Archer nodded and began to read. "Archie—Krauts know your identity, searching for you and the bird. Your people must use caution."

"Krauts?" Papa echoed.

"It's American slang for the Germans," the major replied. "This was written by an American—or someone posing as an American."

"But he thinks that the Nazis know who you are," *Monsieur* Blanc stated.

The pilot nodded. "If so, then we have to be doubly cautious. They'll be anxious to get their hands on the classified information that I possess, and I can't say that I'd care to go through one of their debriefing sessions right now."

Monsieur Blanc took off his glasses. "We had better cut down on the number of searchers," he said. "Most of our men have managed to avoid the German troops so far, but they did catch two of our men and took them down to headquarters for questioning. The men played innocent, and the Nazis released them without incident, but it may not be that easy next time. We'll have to be careful."

Major Archer nodded in agreement. "But here's what gets me—look who sent this message! It is signed 'RV4'!"

Monsieur Marceau shrugged. "So who is RV4?"

"RV4 is the code name for a legendary agent who is known internationally," the pilot continued. "He's the best of the best! He's working for the Allies, but his identity is unknown even to the Allied leaders. He's often referred to as 'The Phantom' because he seems to have the ability to cross international borders without being caught."

"This guy must be really good," Philipe remarked, his eyes shining with excitement.

Major Archer nodded. "RV4 is said to be a master of surveillance and disguises. He's an expert with weapons and munitions, linguistics, and writing and breaking codes. It was rumored that he was the one who first broke the Nazis' secret code, exposing their strategy to the Allies and forcing them to devise other codes. This man is probably the most skilled espionage agent in the world!"

Monsieur Blanc asked, "What would he be doing here in Messiere?"

Major Archer shook his head. "I don't know. As far as I know, there's nothing of importance in this region that would merit his attention. For the Allies to assign RV4 to this region would be like the Germans sending General Himmler to inspect a barracks."

"Would he have come because of you," Papa asked, "or because of the *Eagle*?"

The pilot laughed, then grimaced in pain. "You flatter me, *Monsieur*. But I doubt that I, or my Joe Louis project, would merit the attention of a man of his stature."

He looked again at the note in his hand. "I can't quite believe that I'm actually holding a communication from the legendary RV4!"

Papa cleared his throat. "So what about the search for the *Eagle*?"

"Perhaps we should scale back the search a bit," *Monsieur* Blanc suggested. "Use fewer searchers, less chance of discovery by the Nazis."

"But we have to find it before the Nazis do!" Papa protested. "The fewer people searching, the longer it will take!"

"True," Blanc agreed, "but we're going to have to keep a low profile. I'll pick three other men to search tomorrow with the five of us. We'll start back at the quarry and work our way south again. I'll have the other men stay home for a few days."

"But what if the plane is on the other side of the mountain?" Hans asked. "Shouldn't we search the other side at least once?"

"Not if the major's plane was already below the top of the mountain when he was hit," *Monsieur* Blanc replied. "You heard what the major said. He was at eight thousand feet and bailed out at six thousand. The plane will be somewhere below that, so it has to be on this side, somewhere on the lower half of the mountain."

"How high did you say Mount Piedler is?" Hans asked again.

The tall villager sighed as if Hans' questions were annoying him. "Just over sixteen hundred meters. As Major Archer already said, that's over ninety-six hundred feet."

"Wait!" Hans almost shouted. "We're figuring it wrong! A meter is just over three feet, right?"

Monsieur Blanc shrugged. "I don't know. I'm not that familiar with the American measurements." He looked at Major Archer. "Is that right?"

The pilot nodded. "A meter is a little more than three feet."

"Then Mount Piedler is just over forty-eight hundred feet!" Hans exclaimed. "If Major Archer bailed out at six thousand feet, the *Eagle* could have cleared the top of the mountain and crashed on the other side!"

Papa laughed as he looked from one man to another. "He's right, you know."

Major Archer clapped a hand to his forehead. "I know what a meter is, but somehow I must have multiplied by six instead of three." He looked at Hans. "Thanks, lad."

Hans just grinned.

Monsieur Blanc snorted. "Apparently, we all made the same mistake, and it took a boy to set us straight." He thought for a moment.

"What if I talk Doc Nilsson into staying with the major tomorrow," he suggested, "and the five of us, along with *Monsieur* Brisard, search the western slopes of Mount Piedler? We'll have to start early. It'll take us over an hour just to reach the pass."

✈ ✈ ✈

A heavy fog blanketed Mount Piedler as the search party started up the next morning at daybreak. The men carried ropes and climbing gear, a day's supply of food, and tools on the chance that they might find the plane on the western side. As they climbed, the fog became so dense that they could scarcely see a few meters in front of them.

"If we run into any Nazi troops, we'll be right on top of them before we see them," *Monsieur* Brisard worried aloud.

"True," Papa agreed, "but it could also keep them from seeing us."

The trail intersected the mining camp road, and *Monsieur* Blanc, who was in the lead, paused to adjust his load of cutting tools. He suddenly held up one hand as a signal for silence.

The men quietly dropped to a crouching position as they heard the tramp of heavy boots on the gravel road. As they watched, eight pairs of polished black boots passed by, less than five meters from their hiding place. Hans let out his breath slowly. His heart pounded.

Three minutes after the Nazi troops had disappeared into the fog, the men reversed direction and hurried up the canyon trail. They stopped at the hut to drop off food and trade Doc Nilsson for *Monsieur* Marceau, who had spent the night, then continued upward.

The wind began to pick up. "Maybe this fog will move out," *Monsieur* Blanc observed.

After an hour's hard climb, the men reached the summit and set their equipment down to take a rest break. The sun broke through the clouds just then, illuminating the woods with a warm, golden light. The day suddenly seemed bright and cheery.

Monsieur Brisard opened a canteen and took a drink. "I haven't been up here since I was a youth," he commented.

"Climbing is hard work," *Monsieur* Marceau remarked, "and you bankers aren't used to that! Why, old man Blanc and I run up here every morning, just for the exercise! Don't we, Blanc?"

Monsieur Blanc went along with the joke. *"Oui,"* he replied, "and I run it a second time while you go home to rest and recuperate."

The men laughed.

Philipe pointed upward. "Look at those pines," he remarked. "It looks like the tops have all been chopped off with a giant axe!"

Monsieur Blanc spun around. "Where?"

Philipe pointed again. "It's as though someone tried to cut a path through the top of the trees."

Papa jumped to his feet. "Are you men thinking what I'm thinking?"

They rushed down the steep slope, following the swath of topped trees. They paused when they came to a small bluff, but their gaze followed the strange clearing down the side of the mountain.

Philipe pointed. "Look!"

Fifty meters below, the morning sun glinted off the shiny aluminum skin of a fallen airplane. The wreckage lay upside down in a crumpled heap at the edge of a sheer precipice. One wing, still attached to the fuselage, lay touching the slope above the plane. The other wing had been sheered from the plane as the craft cut its swath through the trees, and now rested some thirty meters above it.

Hans stared in awe. "The *Silver Eagle*!" he whispered.

Philipe studied the plane. "That's a P-38 Lightning," he decided. "This has to be the major's plane!"

Monsieur Blanc slapped him on the back. "We found what we came for!" he rejoiced.

"Thank the Lord!" Papa replied.

The group hurried back up to retrieve their gear, and then hiked quickly down to the wreckage. *Monsieur* Blanc called a halt when they were within ten meters.

"The plane is within a hairbreadth of toppling over the edge," he observed. "We can't see the depth of the chasm from here, but it appears to be quite a drop. We need to figure a way to get down to the plane and secure it before it falls over the brink."

Monsieur Marceau pointed. "I'd say the easiest, and perhaps the safest way, would be to walk down the wing," he suggested. "It's almost as if it forms a bridge to the rest of the plane."

Papa frowned. "It'll be mighty risky! Whoever walks that wing takes a fearsome chance of sending the whole thing right over the edge!"

"What if we send a man down with a line around him?" Marceau proposed. "He could carry additional lines down to secure the plane. It would still be risky, but it would afford a small measure of safety."

"Who's the lightest?" Papa asked.

"Philipe is," Hans replied. "He could do it!"

The other boy shrank back from the idea. "I-I'd rather not!" he protested.

Monsieur Blanc laughed. "We won't make you, Son. We'll send one of the men."

"I'm the next lightest!" Hans volunteered. "I'll do it!"

Monsieur Blanc shook his head. "We appreciate your willingness, Hans, but we'll let a man do it. I'm afraid it's too risky for a boy."

"But I'm lighter than any man here!" Hans protested. "If I go, there's less chance of disturbing the plane! And if I have a line tied to me, there's no danger of going over the edge!"

The man shook his head. "If the line snagged on part of the plane, you'd go right over with it," he argued. "We can't risk it." He looked at Hans' father. "Don't you agree?"

Papa shrugged. "Hans is only twelve, but there have been times already when he's done a man's job. If he's willing to do this, I'm willing to let him."

Monsieur Blanc thought it over. "All right," he said finally. "It's your decision. Let's get a line on him."

Moments later, Hans inched his way carefully down toward the plane, clutching the ends of two ropes, while the third was tied securely around him. Three of the men crouched on the steep slope above him, each with the end of one of the lines around a tree. The men carefully played the ropes out to Hans as he advanced toward the plane, but stood ready to snub the lines at the first hint of trouble.

Hans paused as he reached the wingtip. He gingerly placed one foot on the aluminum skin, testing the structure for stability before he committed his full weight to it. The plane didn't move, so he advanced slowly along the wing toward the fuselage.

"Tie one line to the landing gear," *Monsieur* Blanc instructed him, "and the other to the engine cowling. Then we'll toss you a couple more lines."

Hans nodded. Planting one foot against the edge of the crumpled fuselage, he reached toward the landing gear. With a groan of protesting metal, the plane suddenly shifted. Hans froze in place, afraid to move.

"Hans, move back!" Papa shouted. "Your weight is going to overbalance the plane! Move back!"

At that moment, the wingtip rose in the air nearly a meter as the plane shifted position. A screeching, tearing sound rent the stillness of the morning as the plane slid slowly toward the brink of the drop-off.

13

NAZI ENCOUNTER

"Hans!" Papa shouted. "Jump clear!"

Paralyzed by fear, Hans clung desperately to the fuselage of the fighter as the wreckage slid slowly toward the brink of the chasm. The plane stopped abruptly with a lurch that threw Hans off balance. He let out his breath in a long, grateful sigh. The mangled aircraft had moved less than two meters.

Moving slowly and deliberately, Hans tied one of the ropes to the base of the landing gear with two half hitches. "This one's secure," he called. "Tie it off!"

"Done and done!" The reply came a moment later.

"Hans, I don't think one line will hold it securely," *Monsieur* Blanc called, "so move carefully until you have a couple more lines on it! Try to get your next line on the engine cowling."

Hans carefully climbed down from the wing and slowly advanced toward the nose of the plane, leaning against the fuselage for support on the steep slope. He fastened his second line to an exhaust bracket protruding from the engine cowling, and the men on the hillside above him quickly tied off the other end.

The men threw him two more lines, and in the next few minutes he managed to tie one around the tail assembly and the other to a hoist ring at the base of the wing. *Monsieur* Blanc slid down the slope at that point and tied two additional lines to the plane.

"Well done, Hans," *Monsieur* Blanc said.

He turned and gestured to *Monsieur* Marceau. "Bring the tools down," he called, "and two of the lighter lines to use as safety lines. You and I will cut the Joe Louis free."

Hans knelt in front of the aircraft as he examined the muzzle of a cannon protruding from the nose. "Is this the Joe Louis?"

The villager nodded. "*Oui*, I believe that's what we're after."

Hans watched as *Monsieur* Marceau worked his way toward the wreckage, then turned to Hans. "Why don't you wait on the hillside with the others?" he said. "That will give *Monsieur* Marceau and I room to work. There's no reason to risk a third man for this."

Disappointed, Hans nodded and started up the incline. He was secretly pleased that the tall villager had referred to him as "the third man." He took a seat on the rocky slope beside Papa.

Papa put a hand on his shoulder. "Good work, Son. Mama would have been proud." Hans grinned.

It took the two men over an hour to remove the cannon from the wreckage of the upside down fighter. *Monsieur* Blanc used a hacksaw and a pair of metal sheers to cut through the aluminum skin of the nose, creating a huge hole and exposing the cannon assembly. He and *Monsieur* Marceau knelt side by side on the mountainside and worked together to remove the cannon from the supports inside the nose. Finally, the two men lifted the weapon from the wreckage.

"There it is," *Monsieur* Blanc said proudly, "the Joe Louis! This is one weapon that Hitler isn't going to get his hands on!"

He hefted the cannon, balanced it on his shoulder, then struggled up the steep slope with it. When he reached the others, he carefully let the weapon slide to the ground.

Hans placed both hands under one end of the weapon and lifted it off the ground. "It's heavy!" he exclaimed. "It must weigh thirty kilos!"

Blanc nodded. "*Oui*, it is heavy," he agreed, "but we can remove the barrel and mounts before we carry it up the mountainside. That will eliminate about thirty percent of the weight. Major Archer said that we just need the receiver—the main part of the cannon."

"Should we cut the ropes?" *Monsieur* Marceau asked.

But *Monsieur* Blanc shook his head. "Leave them," he replied. "I'd rather sacrifice the ropes than take a chance on someone getting hurt trying to cut them free. Let's just get this thing out of here as quickly as we can."

Fifteen minutes later, the exuberant group hiked back toward the summit of Mount Piedler. Hans had successfully negotiated for the privilege of carrying the cannon receiver first, but he was huffing and puffing with exertion by the time he had climbed a hundred meters.

"I'll be glad to give someone else a turn," he panted.

Monsieur Marceau stepped forward and took the weapon from him. "I'll take a turn at it," he said. "I'm sure that *Monsieur* Brisard will want to take his turn on the downhill side."

"I'm carrying the tools," the banker retorted cheerfully. "And I resent the insinuation that I would shirk my share of the work."

The triumphant group crested the summit and headed down the eastern slope of the mountain. "Won't Major Archer be delighted to see the Joe Louis?" Philipe asked.

Hans nodded happily. "I'm just glad we kept it out of the hands of the Nazis," he said.

Fifteen minutes later, *Monsieur* Blanc called a halt and rested one end of the cannon receiver on the ground. "Let's split up," he suggested, "so that we're less noticeable. Brisard, we've been giving you a hard time, but do you think that you and Hans could carry the Joe Louis the rest of the way to the hut? The rest of us will take various routes back and meet you there."

Brisard nodded. "Surely." He shouldered the cannon, and Hans followed him down the trail. The rest of the search party disappeared in different directions.

Hans was attempting to carry the weapon through a rugged ravine when the banker suddenly stopped. "Wait!" he whispered.

Hans stood still, scarcely daring to breathe. He listened intently, but the only sound he heard was the wind in the treetops. He let out his breath slowly. "What did you hear?" he whispered.

"Nothing," the banker replied in a whisper. "But don't you smell it? Cigarette smoke!"

Hans sniffed the air, then nodded. He glanced about furtively, then pointed. "Look!" he breathed. Two soldiers with their backs turned stood less than forty meters away! "Back the way we came!" *Monsieur* Brisard whispered. "Quietly!"

Hans' heart pounded with fear as he struggled to climb silently back up the steep slope with the heavy weapon. As he neared the top of the ridge, his foot slipped. He lost his balance and fell to one knee in the leaves. He and the banker waited breathlessly, but to their relief, no soldiers came charging up toward them.

"Thank you, Lord!" Hans breathed.

Hans and *Monsieur* Brisard crept back up the mountainside for another two hundred meters, circled around the vicinity of the two Germans, and then continued down the slope. They paused at the edge of a clearing and silently surveyed the area. There was no sign of soldiers, so they quickly crossed.

As they entered the woods on the far side, Hans heard the metallic click of a rifle bolt. His heart sank as he looked over in time to see two green uniforms materialize from behind a thicket. He cringed as both men pointed their rifles at him.

"We'll take that, lad!" one of the soldiers called, grinning as he stepped toward Hans. "I believe you found what we were looking for!"

As Hans lowered the cannon receiver slowly to the ground, the other soldier trained his rifle on *Monsieur* Brisard. "What is your name, neighbor?"

"Brisard," the man answered flatly. "Pierre Brisard."

"Who's the boy?"

"His name is Hans Von Edler," *Monsieur* Brisard replied. "I'd like to ask that you allow him to go his way. If you have to take someone in, take me."

The second soldier laughed as he leaned over to take the cannon from Hans' grasp. "We don't intend to detain either of you," he replied cheerfully. "All we need from you is this little device." Holding his rifle in one hand, he swung the cannon to his shoulder with the other.

"Both of you may go."

The soldiers laughed as Hans and *Monsieur* Brisard walked dejectedly down the trail.

14

THE JOE LOUIS

Neither *Monsieur* Brisard nor Hans said a word as they continued forlornly down the mountainside toward the hideaway hut where the others would gather. Both the boy and the man were keenly aware of the implications of losing the new weapon to the Nazis. If the Third Reich did develop the rapid-fire cannon before the Allied forces, air superiority would continue to belong to the Nazis. This would undoubtedly result in a longer war and more human suffering.

As they reached the hut, *Monsieur* Brisard looked at Hans, sadly shook his head, and then opened the door. Hans followed him inside. The rest of the search party was already there.

"Here are the men we're waiting for!" Papa said cheerfully as Hans closed the door. "This is a day that will make history!"

Monsieur Blanc noticed the somber look on the faces of the latest arrivals and quickly sensed that something was wrong. "What happened?" he asked quickly. "Where's the Joe Louis?"

In answer, *Monsieur* Brisard simply hung his head and looked at the floor. Hans couldn't bring himself to speak.

Philipe stepped close to Hans. "What happened?" he demanded.

"They took . . ." Hans stopped and swallowed hard, then tried again. "Two soldiers caught us in the woods. They took the Joe Louis."

In spite of his injuries, Major Archer tried to sit up in bed. "The Joe Louis is gone?" he asked. "No! It can't be!"

Hans nodded miserably. "They took it at gunpoint. There was nothing we could do!"

Monsieur Blanc struck his right fist into his left hand angrily. "We never should have split up! With six of us—"

"That wouldn't have changed a thing," *Monsieur* Brisard interrupted. "They were armed and undoubtedly would have shot us if we resisted."

Major Archer let out a sigh of exasperation. "Well, it's done now," he said, "and there's nothing we can do about it." He shook his head sadly. "I had hoped it wouldn't end this way."

Monsieur Blanc seemed to wilt as he dejectedly took a seat on the little stool. "We've let you down, Major," he said quietly. "What can we say?"

Major Archer held up his hands. "You did your best, men. What more can we ask? The tragedy of this is what it's going to mean as the Jerries maintain their air superiority unchallenged."

Blanc suddenly clenched a fist determinedly. "There's just one thing to do!" he declared. "We'll take the Joe Louis back!"

Major Archer shook his head. "What are you going to do, *Monsieur*? What weapons will we use against a whole regiment? The entire village wouldn't stand a chance against the Germans!"

"We'll sneak into their headquarters and retrieve it!" the tall villager asserted. "I'll take volunteers, and we'll do it tonight!"

But the pilot shook his head again. "It won't work, *Monsieur* Blanc. We don't even know where they've taken it. It would be like looking for a grain of rice in a wheat field."

"What about the cannon barrel?" Hans asked. "We left it lying up there by the wreckage of the plane."

The major shook his head. "It doesn't matter. The Nazis can't learn any secrets from it. The crucial thing was the receiver of the Joe Louis. And now it's gone!"

Monsieur Marceau pulled four rusty bolts from the pocket of his heavy coat. "I'm afraid this is all we have left of the Joe Louis," he said. He held out his hand with the bolts in his palm. "Anyone care for a souvenir?"

Major Archer looked at the bolts and came to life. "Give me one of those!" he demanded. The rest of the little group stared at the pilot as *Monsieur* Marceau handed him a bolt.

"Where did you get these?" Major Archer asked, as he examined the bolt.

Monsieur Marceau seemed puzzled by the American's sudden interest. "I guess I stuck them in my pocket when Blanc and I unbolted the Joe Louis."

The pilot shook his head. "These didn't come from the Joe Louis!"

He looked at *Monsieur* Blanc. "The Joe Louis was mounted in the nose of the plane," he said. "It was the cannon on the right. Was that the weapon you retrieved?"

Blanc nodded. "That's the one."

Major Archer's shoulders sagged. "For a moment, I was hoping you had taken one of the old Lewis guns by mistake."

"Wait!" Hans shouted. "The *Eagle* was upside down! You and *Monsieur* Marceau weren't working on the right cannon! It was the left! The plane was upside down!"

The major perked up again. "Quick—tell me," he demanded, "what color was the cannon you removed?"

"What color?" *Monsieur* Blanc said. He shrugged. "It was dark—gun metal blue, I guess you'd say."

"That wasn't the Joe Louis!" the pilot declared eagerly. "The Joe Louis was the color of raw steel; we hadn't blued it yet!" He laughed. "You took out an old Lewis gun!"

"And the Nazis have it now!" Papa exclaimed. "But they think it's the new weapon!"

The group laughed uproariously.

"The Nazi commander is probably radioing Berlin right now," *Monsieur* Brisard chuckled. He pantomimed holding a radio microphone to his mouth and did his best imitation of a German accent. "*Ja*, General Himmler, *ve haf ze* new American weapon right now! But *ve haf* no ammunition!"

Hilarious laughter filled the tiny hut.

"I hope those two Nazi soldiers get a promotion," *Monsieur* Brisard went on. "It will be a temporary one, but they deserve something for their efforts!"

The men laughed again.

Major Archer suddenly grew serious. "There may be trouble ahead," he said soberly. "The Nazis know that you have found the *Eagle*. It won't be long before they figure out that they don't have our new rapid-fire cannon, and they'll come looking for the crew that found the plane. The whole situation could be dangerous for the entire village of Messiere."

He paused and looked from one man to another. "We have to retrieve the Joe Louis, and we have to get it out of the country, fast. Are you men willing to try again tomorrow?"

Monsieur Blanc spoke up. "*Monsieur* Marceau and I will go. The job will only take two of us, and there's no need to put any more than that at risk. We can have the Joe Louis back here in three hours."

Major Archer nodded. "Sounds good to me."

Monsieur Brisard turned to *Monsieur* Blanc. "It's my turn to take the night shift. Why not leave the tools here tonight and pick them up on your way up the mountain?"

Blanc shook his head. "Go on home tonight. I'll stay. That way I won't have to hike back up here in the morning. You can take my turn next time."

Philipe stopped by the Dubois farm the next morning as the two families were eating breakfast. "Did you hear the news?" he asked when Hans came to the door. "*Monsieur* Brisard was taken by the Nazis last night as he was going home from the hut. Nobody's seen him since!"

Hans was stunned by the news. "That's not good at all," he replied. "They'll recognize him as the one with the old Lewis gun, so they'll know that he was at the wreckage! They'll torture him to learn the location of the *Eagle* so they can get the real Joe Louis!"

Philipe nodded. "That's what *Monsieur* Marceau was afraid of. He left before daylight to return to the wreckage and retrieve it before the Nazis have a chance."

"Papa and I are going to work on the barn this morning with *Monsieur* Dubois," Hans said. "Why don't we go see Major Archer this afternoon, if Papa will let me go? Maybe they'll have the Joe Louis there. I'd like to see it."

"All right," Philipe agreed. "I'll stop by at one o'clock. Will that suit you?"

☦ ☦ ☦

"Can—can I ask you something, Philipe?" Hans asked as they hurried up Mount Piedler. Hans nervously licked his lips. His mouth seemed dry, and he realized that his hands were actually trembling. Why was it hard to try to witness to a friend? He knew that God wanted him to do it, and yet, it was hard to get up the courage!

"Sure," Philipe answered, giving Hans a sidelong glance. "What is it?"

"Have—have you ever asked Jesus to be your Savior? I mean, are you saved? Do you know that you're going to heaven?"

Philipe stopped dead in the middle of the trail. "Nobody's ever asked me that before," he replied.

"But have you?" Hans persisted. "Have you ever been saved?" He took a deep breath. There—the question was out, but he was still nervous.

"*Oui,* I have," Philipe answered. "One afternoon I did ask Jesus to save me."

"When was it?" Hans questioned. "And where was it?"

"We were in Paris," Philipe replied. "Papa had taken Colette and me to an exposition. I think we had just turned seven. Anyway, there was a man out on the sidewalk, drawing pictures on a big sketch-board and telling stories from the Bible."

Philipe laughed. "I wanted to stop and hear the story, but Papa and Colette didn't. I started to cry, so Papa agreed to let me stay to listen while he and Colette went to get candy apples. It was a decision I never regretted."

"What happened?" Hans asked.

"The sidewalk artist was drawing a picture of heaven," Philipe continued. "But after telling what a wonderful place heaven was, he said that we couldn't go there because of the bad things we've done. That really upset me! He recited a saying from the Bible, something about being sinners and being too short for God."

"For all have sinned, and come short of the glory of God," Hans quoted.

Philipe stopped and stared at Hans in astonishment. "That's it!" he exclaimed. "How did you know that?"

"It's a Bible verse," Hans explained. "Romans 3:23."

Philipe shook his head. "Today is the first time I've heard that Bible saying since that day on the sidewalk in Paris. When we got home, I tried to find it in the big Bible at the front of the church. But of course, I didn't even know where to look, so I couldn't find it. I asked the minister, but he didn't know what I was talking about."

He picked up a stick from the trail and continued walking. "Anyway, the man then told the story of how Jesus died on the cross so that our sins could be forgiven and we could go to heaven. When I heard the part about Jesus coming back to life, I got so excited that I actually clapped my hands. The man saw it, and it made him laugh. Then he recited a part from the Bible about God loving us sinners so much that Jesus died for us."

"Romans 5:8," Hans quoted. "But God commendeth his love toward us, in that, while we were yet sinners, Christ died for us."

"That's it!" Philipe replied. He stopped again and stared at Hans. "Do you know the whole Bible?"

Hans laughed. "No, just some small parts here and there."

"Oh." Philipe thought for a moment. "Do you know the part about God wanting to give us a gift of long-lasting life?"

Hans thought for a moment. "Is this it? 'For the wages of sin is death, but the gift of God is eternal life, through Jesus Christ our Lord.' That's Romans 6:23."

Philipe grinned and nodded his head. "That's the saying! Anyway, when the man explained those words and told us we could be forgiven, I asked Jesus to forgive me. I got down on my knees right beside a lamp post and asked Jesus to save me!"

The boy's eyes were shining with excitement. "When Papa and Colette came back, I tried to tell them what I had done, but I don't think they understood. Hans, you're the first person I've ever talked to that knew what I was talking about."

Hans was surprised. "In our village in Austria, a lot of people knew the Lord."

Philipe shook his head. "Not here. Even Papa didn't know."

Hans was silent for a moment as they hiked. Finally, he asked, "What about Colette? Has she been saved?"

Philipe shook his head. "I don't think so, Hans. And I didn't really know how to tell her." His voice choked as he said, "I've asked God to send someone to tell her like the man in Paris told me, but no one ever has. Can you tell her?"

Hans wasn't sure how to answer. "I-I think Gretchen will," he said finally. "But she's afraid that Colette won't listen to her."

"Oh, but she will," Philipe assured him. "I know she will."

Gretchen thinks that Colette hates her," Hans confided, "especially after what happened yesterday."

Philipe sighed. "Mama said that Colette came home in tears yesterday. She kept sobbing, 'I killed Gretchen. I killed Gretchen.' Mama said she was so upset she couldn't even talk. Mama had no idea what had happened until your father came and told her."

He turned to Hans with a pleading look on his thin face. "Please tell Gretchen that my sister will listen. Please ask her to tell Colette how to be saved."

Hans nodded. "I will," he promised, "but I know that Gretchen is afraid." He swatted at a bush beside the trail. "Why is Colette so hateful?"

Philipe let out a long sigh. "She's been that way ever since Papa died. She was close to Papa, Hans—awfully close. When he died, I think it tore her heart out. She hasn't been the same since."

"But why the meanness?" Hans questioned. "Even to poor Klause! She acts like she would like to kill him!"

Philipe hesitated. "She's treated him that way ever since she found out he was deaf."

Hans was perplexed. "Huh? What's that got to do with it? You don't treat deaf people that way just because they're deaf!"

"Papa was deaf, Hans. That's why he was killed. One of the workers shouted a warning just before the explosives went off. Everyone ran clear but Papa. He never heard the warning."

"I still don't understand," Hans replied. "What's that got to do with Klause? Why would Colette treat him that way?"

"I think . . ." Philipe stopped, searching for words. "It's almost like she's jealous of Klause. He's deaf, like Papa was, but he's still alive, and Papa's not. So Colette resents him. Does that make sense?"

Hans smiled sadly. "*Oui,* in a way it does. And then again, it doesn't."

"Ask Gretchen to talk to her, will you? I want Colette to know how to be saved. She's not a bad person, Hans. But she's hurting inside, and that's the reason she acts the way she does."

Hans nodded. "I will, Philipe."

Philipe grabbed his arm. "Hans," he said softly, "I'm sorry for what Colette has done to Gretchen. And down inside, I think Colette is, too."

Just as the trail dipped down into the ravine below the hut, the boys heard voices. Hans and Philipe both dropped to the ground and crawled to the concealment of a nearby thicket. Hans raised up on one knee. What he saw made his heart pound with fear.

Monsieur Blanc and *Monsieur* Marceau stood in a small gully twenty or thirty meters away with their hands raised over their heads. A shiny, cylindrical object that Hans recognized immediately as the rapid-fire cannon lay in the leaves at their feet, and three Nazi soldiers stood aiming two rifles and a machine gun at the men's hearts!

15

THE CHALLENGE

Hans and Philipe dropped to the ground behind the thicket, terrified by what they had just seen. "The Nazis are going to get the Joe Louis, Philipe!" Hans whispered. "We've got to stop them!"

Philipe shook his head. "There's nothing we can do!" He whispered back. "It's two of us against two rifles and a machine gun!"

"Down on your knees, *Messieurs*!" one of the soldiers barked.

Horrified, Hans rose up on one knee to see what was happening. The Nazi soldiers were aiming their weapons at the backs of the two villagers. "Philipe, they're going to kill them!" Hans groaned. "We have to do something!"

At that instant, three shots rang out nearby, followed by the explosion of a grenade. All three soldiers whirled around. "What was that?" one soldier exclaimed.

"It's not our troops!" another answered. "Let's get out of here with this thing!" He stooped, hefted the Joe Louis to his shoulder, and then dashed down the trail, followed by one of his companions.

The third soldier hesitated. He turned and smashed *Monsieur* Marceau between the shoulder blades with the butt of his rifle, knocking the villager face down in the leaves, and then dashed after his fellow soldiers.

"Marceau, are you all right?" *Monsieur* Blanc asked his companion, who struggled shakily to his feet.

"*Oui,* I'll live," Marceau answered, "but tomorrow I'll have a bruise the size of a cantaloupe."

"Come on, Philipe," Hans whispered, "let's follow the soldiers and see where they take the Joe Louis!"

The two boys slipped from their hiding place and, heedless of the danger, darted down the trail after the soldiers. *We have to keep them in sight to find out where they're taking it,* Hans told himself, *but somehow make sure that they don't see us.*

Hans and Philipe raced around a bend in the trail to come face to face with Klause, who was just pulling a narrow, two-wheeled cart loaded with wood onto the trail. Hans darted to one side to avoid a collision with the cart, and Philipe did the same. The woodcutter stared in bewildered astonishment as they passed.

The boys ran over the crest of a small ridge and then tried to check their speed as the trail dropped sharply into a steep ravine. Hans lost his footing and fell forward, skidding on his arms and chest down the abrupt incline. Philipe, unable to stop in time, stumbled over him and fell also.

"Halt!" a gruff voice snapped.

The boys looked up to find themselves staring into the muzzle of a machine gun five meters away as the two soldiers with rifles walked forward to join their companion. The soldier who had clubbed *Monsieur* Marceau raised his rifle to his cheek and drew a bead on Hans.

"Don't shoot!" muttered the grenadier who was carrying the Joe Louis. "Let's just get back to headquarters with this thing."

"Get out of here," the man with the machine gun ordered. He gestured back up the incline with the muzzle of the weapon. "Now!"

The terrified boys scrambled back up the incline as fast as they could go, and the soldiers laughed.

Hans and Philipe ran nearly two hundred meters up the steep slope. Hans glanced over his shoulder and then came to a stop to catch his breath. Sides heaving, he stood with his hands on his knees. "That was close!" he panted.

As the pounding of his heart subsided, Hans looked around to realize that they were standing in the spot where they had nearly collided with the woodcutter. "Where's Klause?" he wondered aloud. "He was right here just a moment ago!"

Philipe shrugged. "He seems to appear and disappear like a leprechaun!"

Hans frowned. "Why would he be cutting wood this far up the mountain?" he wondered aloud. "It's very steep, and he'd have to cart the wood so far."

Philipe just shook his head. "There's no telling, Hans. Klause is a strange one, and his mind isn't all there."

Moments later the boys approached the hut, paused to be certain that they were not being followed, and then hurried inside. *Monsieur* Blanc and *Monsieur* Marceau leaped to their feet as the boys entered and then sank back down when they saw who had come.

"Boys, I'm afraid I have bad news," Major Archer said from his bed. "The Joe Louis was taken!"

Hans and Philipe nodded dejectedly. "We saw it happen," Hans replied. "Three soldiers. We were afraid they were going to shoot *Monsieur* Blanc and *Monsieur* Marceau!"

"We thought so, too," *Monsieur* Blanc stated. "I think they would have except there were gunshots and an explosion."

"What caused that?" Philipe asked. "We heard it, too."

The two men shook their heads. "We have no idea," Blanc said. "But it was mighty close. It was almost as though someone was trying to create a diversion to save us."

"Well, whatever it was, it worked out for good," Major Archer remarked. "I'm just thankful you men weren't killed." He sighed. "Now we have to determine if there's anything to be done about the Joe Louis."

"We'll get it back," *Monsieur* Marceau declared. "Whatever it takes, we'll get it back."

The American smiled. "I appreciate your enthusiasm, *Monsieur*, but it won't be that easy. We have no idea even where it is at this moment."

"They're taking it to headquarters," Philipe blurted.

The three men looked at him. "How do you know that, Philipe?" Major Archer asked.

"We followed them," Philipe replied. "One of the soldiers told the others to hurry so that they could get it back to headquarters."

"You followed the soldiers?" *Monsieur* Blanc echoed, shaking his head. "Do you realize how dangerous that could have been? They might have killed you!"

"We thought they were going to," Hans muttered.

"Boys, listen to me," the tall villager urged. "Don't ever try a thing like that again. If there's any shadowing to be done, one of the men will take care of it, all right?"

Both boys nodded.

The men sat quietly thinking the situation through. Philipe and Hans sank to seats on the floor and waited.

"What if we send Hans into town to get his papa and Doc Nilsson?" Major Archer suddenly suggested. "They both have good heads on their shoulders. We can brainstorm this thing and see if we can come up with a plan of action. There has to be a way to save the Joe Louis!"

Blanc nodded. "Sounds good to me," he agreed.

Hans stood to his feet.

"Take your time, Hans," Blanc cautioned. "Keep it quiet and don't do anything to attract attention. And watch out for the soldiers and SS troops."

Hans nodded and headed for the door.

"Be careful, Son," Major Archer called.

As Hans hurried down the mountain trail, he decided to take the path that ran along the edge of the canyon because it would be shorter and faster. Besides, there would be less of a chance of running into any soldiers.

When he reached the Dubois farm, he found Papa and *Monsieur* Dubois working on the roof of the barn. He scrambled up the ladder and carefully crept across the steep roof to crouch beside his father. *Monsieur* Dubois knelt just three meters away, energetically swinging a hammer.

"Papa, they want you at the hut," Hans whispered. "It's important!"

Papa slipped his hammer into his tool belt and removed two nails from his mouth. "What happened?"

"The Nazis got the Joe Louis," Hans whispered. "The real one! Major Archer wants you there to help decide what to do."

Papa thought it over. "All right," he said. "I'll see if *Monsieur* Dubois will let me go. I have to admit, he's been very understanding."

Hans hurried into town and notified Doc Nilsson, who readily agreed to come. "Give me just a moment to get my coat and tell my wife," he told Hans, "and I'll hike up with you."

Hans and the doctor entered the hut to find that Hans' father was already there. Papa, the villagers and Major Archer were discussing the rapid-fire cannon and the possibility of safely retrieving it from the Nazis.

"But there's no way to know for certain that the Joe Louis is really at the Nazi headquarters," Papa was saying.

"We're relatively certain that it is," Major Archer replied. "The boys heard one of the grenadiers planning to take it there."

"Well, that would be the most logical place for it," *Monsieur* Marceau said. "But we can't just shoot our way in and snatch it from under their noses! We wouldn't make it out of there alive."

The pilot nodded. "I think everyone will agree that's out of the question. But we have to get the Joe Louis back!

We need to come up with a plan of action. If anyone has any ideas, I'm open to them."

Doc Nilsson said, "What if we were to offer a bribe to one of the Nazis in return for information? You know, find out for sure if the cannon is really there, and where they're keeping it."

"Possibly," *Monsieur* Blanc replied. "But then we also run the risk of alerting them that we're after it."

Papa frowned. "There has to be some way of finding out where it is. Then we could decide just how to go about getting it back."

The door opened just then, and *Monsieur* Brisard stepped in and quietly closed the door. He was greeted with exclamations of surprise and relief.

"Brisard!" Marceau laughed, "we thought they decided to keep you."

The banker turned around, and the room suddenly grew silent. *Monsieur* Brisard's face was swollen and puffy, and both his eyes were swollen nearly shut. His lips were cracked and bleeding.

"Pierre!" Blanc cried out, "what did they do to you?"

Pierre Brisard waved one hand. "I'm all right," he assured the group. "They worked me over last night and then again this morning. They were trying to get me to reveal the location of the plane because they were certain we had found it." He laughed, then clutched his side. "But they didn't get a thing out of me. No, *Monsieur*! Not a thing!"

"We're just glad you're alive," Doc Nilsson said quietly.

"Don't worry about me," Brisard replied. "I'll be all right. Here's the important thing—they got the Joe Louis!"

The men nodded soberly. "We know."

Major Archer held up one hand. "Wait, *Monsieur* Brisard. How did you know that they had the cannon?"

"They had me upstairs this afternoon for another session of interrogation," the man replied. "I was in the room where *Monsieur* Jayet had his showroom. It's a spacious, elegant room, with the huge jeweler's safe right beside the fireplace.

"Anyway, three officers came rushing in just as my interrogation was about to begin. They were so excited that I don't think they realized that I was there. They had the Joe Louis with them! They put it in the safe so it would be secure until tomorrow when they're expecting a delegation of high-ranking officers. After tomorrow, the Joe Louis will be on its way to Berlin."

Major Archer shook his head. "How did you learn all that?"

"I speak a little German," Brisard answered, "and as I said, I don't think the three officers even knew I was there. They were chattering away like a bunch of old women. They expect to receive promotions as a reward for capturing the cannon."

Major Archer struggled to a sitting position. "Good work, *Monsieur* Brisard! RV4 himself couldn't have done better!"

Brisard grinned, then held a hand against his injured lip.

"You heard what he said," the pilot said, looking from one man to another. "The Joe Louis goes to Berlin tomorrow! If we want it back, it's tonight or never! Now that we know for certain where it is, I guess we're back to the original question: does anyone have any ideas how to go about getting it back?"

"We'd have to blow the safe," one man said. "*Monsieur* Jayet was the only one who knew the combination. He didn't even trust his wife with it!"

"That's out of the question," Blanc retorted. "We'd have a hundred armed Nazis on our hands before the door hit the floor! There has to be another way."

"Does anybody care to recommend a good safe-cracker?" Major Archer asked, and the men laughed at his feeble attempt at humor.

A loud thud echoed through the tiny hut as an object struck the door, causing the occupants to jump. *Monsieur* Blanc leaped to his feet and cautiously opened the door. Frowning, he stepped outside.

He was back in a moment with a large piece of aspen bark. "This was lying just outside the door," he said. "but look what's on it!"

The group crowded close as he turned the section of bark over. A message had been scratched into the inside surface of the wood. "What does it say?" Philipe asked.

Monsieur Blanc shook his head. "It doesn't make any sense whatever," he replied. He lifted the bark closer to his own face. "Here's what it says: R38L53R42L17." He looked up. "What kind of a message is that?"

"I know what it is!" Papa declared. "It's the combination to a safe. *Monsieur* Jayet's safe!"

Monsieur Blanc's eyes grew wide. "I believe you're right, Gustav!" A puzzled look crossed his face. "Now how in the world did this get here? Here we are discussing ways to get into the safe, and someone delivers the combination to our door! This is uncanny!"

"I think I have an idea," Major Archer said. "RV4!"

Blanc shook his head. "But this is impossible, *Monsieur*! Nobody could do this!"

The pilot laughed. "That's why I believe it's from RV4," he replied. "This is precisely his style!"

He looked from one man to another. "You men know what we're up against. If we're to recover the Joe Louis, we have to do it tonight. But anyone entering Nazi headquarters to make the attempt will be risking his life. Are any of you willing to volunteer?"

16

RECOVERY ATTEMPT

The wind howled and gusted outside the secluded hut as the little group sat silently considering Major Archer's request. Finally, Papa spoke up. "I'll go," he said, "if *Monsieur* Marceau will accompany me."

Monsieur Blanc nodded in approval. "You two would be the best for the mission," he said. "You're both rugged, athletic men, and you both have good heads on your shoulders." He turned to Marceau. "How's your back?"

The other man flexed his shoulders. "I'm going to be sore tomorrow, but I'm all right. I'm your man."

"I'll go, too!" Hans offered.

Blanc shook his head. "This is a job for the men, Hans. But we appreciate your offer."

"But you'll need a lookout," Hans persisted. "Someone to watch for trouble while the men are inside the hotel. I can do that!"

"You're right, we will need a lookout," Blanc conceded, "but we'll use a man for that, Son."

"Wait," Papa interjected. "Think about it. Using a boy for a lookout just might make sense. The Nazis would be less likely to notice a boy, rather than an adult."

Blanc shrugged. "You might have something there."

"I'm willing," Hans said again.

Major Archer laughed. "I think you've got the job, Hans."

"So what's our plan of action?" Marceau asked.

"The Widow Benoit's house is adjacent to the hotel," Blanc told the group. "Miriam Benoit is a sweet old saint, but she's also trustworthy and can keep her mouth closed. I suggest that we go down there and look over the situation from inside her house. We could see the eastern side of the hotel from one of her upstairs windows without the Nazis realizing that we're up to something."

"What are we waiting for?" Papa asked, rising to his feet and pulling on his coat. "Time's slipping away."

"Good luck," Major Archer told the men. "I appreciate you men putting your lives on the line."

Hans opened the door and stared in surprise. The air was filled with swirling masses of white, and a blanket of glistening snow covered the ground, trees, and bushes. "It's snowing!" he called to the others. "There's already two or three centimeters on the ground!"

Philipe stayed with Major Archer as Hans and the four men slipped from the hut and headed down toward the village in two groups. The falling snow filled the air and swirled about their faces, making it difficult to see the trail.

Monsieur Blanc paused to brush out their tracks at the point where the trail intersected the road. "Not that it matters," he told the others. "This snow is falling so fast it will fill our tracks in five minutes."

Forty minutes later, *Madame* Benoit showed her unexpected visitors to an upstairs bedroom. "You get a good view of the hotel from either of these windows," she told them. "What a shame that such a grand old place should be swarming with those murderous Nazis! They come and go as if they own the village. They haven't bothered me yet, but I must admit, I am afraid of them."

"*Oui, Madame,*" *Monsieur* Blanc replied in response to the old woman's remarks. "Nazis never make good neighbors."

Madame Benoit turned toward the stairs. "Stay as long as you like," she told *Monsieur* Blanc. "I'll be downstairs."

The men crowded to the two windows to study the old hotel now being used as the headquarters for the Nazi troops. The eastern wall of the stately stone building was less than seven meters away. A row of crystalline icicles hung from the eaves, and an ancient oak stood in the narrow space between the two buildings, its gnarled branches now frosted with snow. The snowstorm increased in fury, nearly obscuring the hotel from view.

"There was a sentry at the front door," *Monsieur* Blanc remembered. "But he can't see this end of the building, so I think we're safe."

Papa chuckled. "He may not stay out there long in this weather."

Blanc turned to *Monsieur* Brisard. "Which windows are the showroom where the safe is?"

Brisard silently studied the windows for a moment or two. "The window on the end is a small room by itself," he replied finally. "That's where they kept me last night. The next three windows are the fireplace room, and that's where they have the safe."

"What is that room?" *Monsieur* Blanc asked, pointing to the end of the building where a single story jutted out from the rest of the two-story building.

"That used to be a storage room," *Monsieur* Marceau interjected. "I've done some carpentry work for *Monsieur* Jayet, and that's where he kept tools and equipment."

"The roof of the storage room is just below the end window," Blanc pointed out. "If we could gain access to the roof, we could reach the window easily."

"That window has a broken lock!" Marceau said excitedly. "I was always after *Monsieur* Jayet to let me replace it, but he wasn't concerned because it's a second-story window."

"That's our way in," Blanc decided. "Now we simply have to figure a way to access the roof. I'm afraid a ladder would be out of the question—it could be spotted too easily."

"What if we throw a grappling hook up into that tree," Hans suggested, "with a line attached? Then Papa and *Monsieur* Marceau can just swing across from this window to the roof."

The men studied the tree as they considered Hans' suggestion. "I can do it," Marceau stated, turning to Papa, "if you can."

Papa nodded. "It shouldn't be too difficult, except for the ice and snow."

"We'll post Hans out in the street," Blanc decided, "where he can watch the sentry and you can still see him from the window. He'll signal when the coast is clear and warn you if trouble develops."

He surveyed the yard between the two buildings for a moment and then turned to Hans. "We'll wait till dark, of course, but once the men are in position, you'll come walking down the street. If it's safe for the men to proceed, you'll take off your hat and shake it as if you're getting snow out of it."

"What if I spot someone coming?" Hans asked. "How will I warn Papa and *Monsieur* Marceau?"

"You'll have a sudden coughing spell," the man told him. "That would alert the men without giving the whole thing away."

Hans nodded to show that he understood.

"Now," Blanc continued, "both you men need to memorize the combination to the safe."

Brisard came into the room just then. "I was down talking with *Madame* Benoit," he told the others. "She says that they turn out the lights upstairs at ten o'clock every night. She doesn't think they use the fireplace room for sleeping quarters."

"*Oui*, that's good," Blanc replied. "Then we meet here at eleven. I'll bring the grappling hook, a line, and a small flashlight. We'll just hope for the best."

The men trooped downstairs. *Monsieur* Blanc told the elderly homeowner of their plans to return that night and stressed the need for secrecy. The men thanked her, then hurried out into the snowstorm.

The snow was nearly twenty centimeters deep as Hans and Papa trudged toward *Madame* Benoit's house. The storm had not yet abated, and the fierce wind and falling snow covered their tracks as quickly as they made them. Beams of silver moonlight glistened on the snow, creating a scene of breath-taking beauty.

Hans shivered. "I'm afraid for you, Papa," he said quietly. "The idea of you going into the Nazi headquarters scares the life out of me."

His father nodded. "Me, too," he admitted. "But I'm trying to leave the situation in the hands of God and trust Him for the outcome."

Hans kicked at a snow-covered shrub. "Sometimes it's hard to trust, isn't it?"

Papa coughed and pulled his fur hat lower over his ears. "That it is, Son. That it is."

They paused in the shadow of *Madame* Benoit's house to check up and down the street, and then slipped up on the porch. *Monsieur* Blanc opened the door before they had time to knock. "Come on in," he whispered. "Marceau just got here."

Hans' heart was pounding with anticipation as he followed Papa upstairs. A coiled line with a grappling hook at one end lay on the polished hardwood floor beneath the window nearest the hotel.

"I'll have you carry the Joe Louis," Blanc told Papa, "so I'll make you a harness to carry it on your back. That will keep your hands free for climbing."

Papa raised his arms as the villager fashioned a harness from light rope by crisscrossing it across his chest, under his arms, and across his back. When Blanc was finished, two loops of cord hung just beneath Papa's shoulders. "Slip the Joe Louis through these, then tie the ends together to hold it in place," he told Marceau.

Papa took a deep breath, then expelled it nervously. "I think we're ready."

"Do you know the combination to the safe?" Blanc asked him.

"Right thirty-eight, left fifty-three, right forty-two, left seventeen," Papa recited.

"You got it," Blanc replied. "Remember, it's four complete turns to the right before you stop at thirty-eight, three complete turns to the left before stopping at fifty-three, and two complete turns on the last two numbers. Archer thinks that's standard for that type of safe, but if that doesn't do it, you'll have to experiment."

Blanc looked at Marceau. "Let's hear the combination from you." The man recited it perfectly.

"Hans," *Monsieur* Blanc said, "they'll be ready in two minutes. Walk east to the end of the block, wait thirty seconds, then walk back. Stop at the point between the buildings where you can see the sentry at the front door of the hotel. If all seems well, give the signal.

"Once the men are inside the hotel, continue on around the block, then slip into the bushes in front of the house. When the men reappear at the window, step out and give the same signal."

Hans nodded. "I understand."

Moments later, the moon slipped behind a cloud as Hans strode down the street. His heart pounded with fear. *What if the Nazis catch Papa and Monsieur Marceau?*

Hans stopped at the point where he could see the sentry standing in the shadows by the hotel entrance. A tiny red glow told him that the soldier was smoking a cigarette. Hans glanced up and down the street, then casually took off his hat and shook it in front of him.

He glanced over just in time to see a dark body swing noiselessly in an arc from the window of the widow's house to the roof of the hotel storage room. He smiled. *Monsieur* Marceau had done it perfectly.

The smile faded as the villager on the roof struggled to get a foothold on the slippery shingles, lost his balance, and slid over the edge to land in the snow with a soft grunt. Hans looked in the direction of the sentry and then hurried to the spot where his friend had fallen.

"*Monsieur* Marceau!" he called softly, "are you all right?"

A groan of pain gave him his answer. "It's my ankle," Marceau replied through clenched teeth. "I think I sprained it!"

"I'll help you back to the widow's house," Hans told the man in a whisper. "Can you stand up?"

"Check the street first," Marceau replied. "Make sure that no one heard me fall."

Hans hurried back to the street, thankful for the clouds that still blocked most of the moon's light. He looked in the direction of the hotel entrance, and his heart froze. The red glow of the sentry's cigarette bobbed up and down in the darkness as the soldier strode purposefully straight toward him!

Lord, help us! Hans cried silently. Remembering the signal, he bent over in a sudden fit of loud coughing.

17

THE REPLACEMENT

"What are you doing here, *knabe*?" the Nazi soldier demanded. He plucked the stub of the cigarette from his own lips and hurled it into a snowdrift, then blew a cloud of irritating smoke directly in Hans' face. "Answer me!"

Hans struggled to think of an explanation that would satisfy the sentry. He knew he couldn't lie to the man, and yet, if the Nazi discovered their mission, Hans and *Monsieur* Marceau would possibly both face death. *Lord, he prayed desperately, give me an answer!*

The soldier prodded Hans in the chest with the muzzle of his rifle. "What are you doing here?" he asked again.

"I-I'm just . . ." Hans stammered, searching for an answer.

"Open your coat!"

"W-What?"

"I said, open your coat!" The soldier was growing more and more impatient.

Hans slowly unbuttoned the front of his heavy coat. His gaze wandered to the yard between the buildings, and he was thankful to realize that it was too dark for the Nazi to see his tracks across the snow or the dark form of *Monsieur* Marceau slumped against the side of the building.

To Hans' surprise, the sentry took one hand from his rifle to frisk Hans quickly. "Nothing," the man said as if he were disappointed.

Placing the barrel of his rifle under Hans' chin, the soldier slowly pushed upward until Hans' head was tilted back at an uncomfortable angle. "Are you the one who has been stealing food from our mess supplies?"

"No, *Monsieur*!" Hans replied.

The pressure of the cold steel increased. "I'm not French, *knabe!*"

"*Nein, Herr* soldier!" Hans blurted. His teeth chattered with cold and fear.

The Nazi soldier leaned close. His face was mere centimeters from Hans', and the smell of tobacco smoke was over-powering. Hans stared at the man in alarm.

The Nazi let out a quiet, scornful laugh, lowered the rifle, and walked toward the hotel without looking back. Hans sighed in relief. "Thank you, Lord," he breathed.

He stood silently for several moments as his heart stopped pounding and his fear subsided. When he was certain that the sentry wasn't coming back, he hurried to *Monsieur* Marceau. "You're a good man, Hans," the villager whispered. "Now help me get back inside the house."

"What happened?" *Monsieur* Blanc asked as he helped Marceau to a seat in *Madame* Benoit's parlor. "It looked to us as though you made it easily, but then you dropped into the snow like a dead sparrow!"

"The roof is very slick," Marceau replied, rubbing his ankle gingerly. "I say the only way to get up there is with a ladder. But I'm afraid this ankle is going to keep me from completing my mission!"

Blanc sighed. "Don't worry about that. We'll find a replacement."

Papa turned to *Madame* Benoit, who hovered nearby. "May we have a bowl for snow for this man's ankle?" he asked. He looked back to Blanc. "I suppose you'll take his place?"

The tall villager shook his head. "I wish I could, but I sometimes suffer from vertigo and easily lose my balance. If I had an attack on the roof, it would be disastrous."

"I'll go, Papa!" Hans volunteered.

Papa looked back to *Monsieur* Blanc. "What do you think?"

The tall villager shook his head. "It's a man's job, Hans. The men that enter that building are walking right into the jaws of death itself."

"I'm willing," Hans said quietly.

"I'm sorry, lad, but it's a job for one of the men."

"You'll lose too much time," Hans argued. "By the time you find one of the other villagers and get him over here . . ."

Blanc sighed and looked at Papa. "Who else knows the combination to the safe?"

"Right thirty-eight, left fifty-three, right forty-two, left seventeen," Hans recited. "See, I know the combination already."

Monsieur Blanc shrugged and looked at Hans, then turned back to Hans' father. "I'll let you make the decision."

Hans waited expectantly while Papa thought it over. Papa glanced toward the hotel, stroked his mustache nervously, and finally turned to Hans. "We say we trust the Lord, *oui*? I suppose that this is one of those times when I'll just have to trust Him. If you're still willing, you may come with me."

Hans grinned. "Thanks, Papa."

❄ ✳ ❄

The snow was falling swiftly as Hans and his father crept across the space between the two buildings. Papa carefully placed the ladder against the eaves of the storage room and then leaned against it to be certain that it was secure. Hans handed him the coil of line with the grappling hook.

"I'll secure the line to the roof of the building," Papa whispered. "But don't come up the ladder until I've reached the peak. I'll wave as a signal. Keep a tight grip on the line for stability as you climb. *Monsieur* Blanc will lay the ladder in the snow until we are ready to return."

Hans held the ladder steady as his father crept up the rungs. His mind raced. *What if the Nazis are watching us right now from one of the windows? What if Papa and I climb through the window right into their hands? What will they do to us?*

Papa threw the grappling hook over the peak of the roof, pulled on the rope to make certain that it held securely, and then started up the icy roof.

Lord, help us, Hans prayed silently.

A loud thump sounded from the direction of the roof, and Hans looked upward. Papa had slipped and fallen. As Hans watched, Papa carefully raised himself to his knees.

Hans' attention was snatched away as a light suddenly winked on in the downstairs window closest to the ladder. The curtains parted as the stern face of a Nazi officer peered out. Hans held his breath. The man was staring right at him!

Using his hand to wipe the frost from the windowpane, the officer pressed his nose against the glass. Hans stood motionless as the Nazi scanned the yard. *Doesn't he see me?* Hans thought. *Doesn't he see the ladder?*

But the officer shrugged and turned away from the window. Moments later, the light winked out. *It was too dark out here for him to see me,* Hans gratefully realized.

He looked up to see that Papa had reached the peak of the roof and was now waving for him to come. The end of the rope came swishing down to land in the snow beside him. Hans climbed the ladder and then gripped the rope tightly with both hands as he stepped carefully onto the icy roof. *Monsieur* Blanc slipped from the shadows of *Madame* Benoit's house, carefully laid the ladder in the snow, then melted into the darkness again.

Pulling himself hand over hand up the rope, Hans crept up the slick shingles until he reached the apex of the roof. Papa already had the window open.

"I'll go first," Papa whispered softly. "Don't move until I motion for you to come through the window. We can't use the light until we get to the safe, so we'll have to move at a snail's pace to keep from bumping into anything."

Hans nodded. His heart seemed to be in his throat. He was trembling, and his fear was so great he could scarcely breathe. Papa put a hand on his shoulder. "God Almighty is with us," he whispered. "We have to trust Him tonight."

The moon darted from behind the clouds just then, bathing the village rooftops in its silvery beams. Papa let out his breath, then ducked through the window. Moments later, he turned and beckoned for Hans to follow him.

Papa and Hans stood motionless in the room, straining their eyes to see in the darkness. As Papa turned and took a step toward the doorway, a low grunt came from just a meter or two away. Father and son stood still, barely breathing, listening intently. As Hans' eyes grew accustomed to the dim light, he could make out the form of a sleeping soldier on a bunk beside the doorway to the fireplace room.

Hans pointed, and Papa nodded silently. Holding his breath, he crept across the room on tiptoe. Hans followed him with heart pounding furiously.

They stepped through the doorway into the spaciousness of the fireplace room, then stood silently surveying the darkness of the room. Hans was relieved to find that there were no soldiers sleeping in the room.

"This way!" Papa whispered. "The safe should be over here." Hans followed him.

Moments later they knelt beside the massive safe. Papa lit a small candle and handed it to Hans. "Hold it close to the dial so I can see," he whispered. "But you watch the door. If you see anyone, pinch the candle out immediately!" To Hans' surprise, Papa pulled Colonel Von Bronne's automatic from inside his coat and carefully laid it on the floor between his feet.

Hans turned his attention to the door as Papa began to spin the dial on the safe. "Right four times to thirty-eight," Papa whispered under his breath. He leaned closer to the dial and turned it more slowly. "Hold the candle a few centimeters lower, Hans."

Papa stopped the dial on the correct number. "Three times left to fifty-seven," he breathed.

Hans turned his attention from the doorway. "Fifty-three, Papa!" he whispered. "Left to fifty-three!"

Papa paused with his hand still on the dial. "Are you sure?"

"It's right thirty-eight, left fifty-three, right forty-two, and left seventeen," Hans whispered. "I'm positive!"

Papa nodded. "I think you're right, Son. We'll try fifty-three." He spun the dial three complete turns to the left, then leaned close as he stopped at fifty-three.

"Right forty-two?"

Hans nodded.

Moments later, Papa stopped the dial at the final number. "Here goes," he whispered. He pulled on the big silver handle, and the door clicked open.

Hans glanced toward the doorway to see a light bobbing up and down on the stairs. "Papa," he whispered urgently, "someone's coming!"

As Hans pinched the candle flame out, Papa reached over and gently pushed the safe door closed again. "Follow me," he whispered. He crawled a few meters beyond the safe and dropped to the floor behind a pile of firewood. Hans followed suit.

The flashlight beam darted around the room as the soldier stepped through the doorway. Hans' heart leaped with fear. Papa had left his gun on the floor in front of the safe, and the Nazi would surely see it!

The beam of the light flashed in their direction, and the soldier stalked toward them.

18

PURSUED!

Hans and his father watched fearfully as the Nazi soldier strode across the room toward the woodpile. Hans held his breath.

The soldier stepped to one of the windows and gazed in the direction of *Madame* Benoit's house. He held his flashlight against the glass of the windowpane as he swept the yard with the beam. Satisfied that nothing was amiss, he turned and walked to a window on the opposite side of the room.

Hans raised up on one knee to watch. Abruptly, the soldier spun around and swept the room with the beam of his flashlight. Hans crouched lower.

The bright beam swept around the room, then back to rest on the door of the safe. Hans waited breathlessly. Could the soldier tell that the door was unlocked?

But the light swung toward the open doorway as the soldier strode from the room. When the man was gone, Papa let out a long sigh. "I was praying like I've never prayed before!" he whispered.

Papa waited in silence for two or three minutes, listening intently. Hans crouched beside him. Finally, Papa slipped from his hiding place and crept toward the safe. Hans followed.

Papa knelt in front of the safe and slowly swung the heavy door open. "We won't light the candle again unless we absolutely need it," he whispered.

Hans knelt beside him.

"Here it is," Papa whispered. He leaned forward and lifted the Joe Louis from the safe. Carefully, he set one end of the rapid-fire cannon on the floor and balanced it upright. Using his free hand, he closed the safe door, turned the handle, and spun the dial.

"We've got it, Hans!" he whispered triumphantly as he leaned over to retrieve his weapon from the floor. "Praise the Lord! Now, let's get out of here!"

Father and son crept across the darkened fireplace room and passed into the small room where the lone soldier slept. Papa handed the Joe Louis to Hans. "Hold this until I get situated out on the roof," he whispered, "then pass it to me. Once we get outside, you can help me get it into my harness."

Hans glanced at the sleeping form on the bunk, but the soldier snored peacefully.

Papa raised the window and crawled through. Hans stepped toward the window, caught his foot on a crack in the floor, and lost his balance. The cannon fell to the floor with a loud crash.

Hans spun around, expecting the sleeping soldier to come to life and leap from his bed. But to Hans' amazement, the man went on sleeping peacefully. *This guy would sleep through an earthquake,* Hans thought.

He bent over and lifted the Joe Louis, cradling it carefully in his arms, and, with great effort, passed it through the window to his father. Papa set the heavy weapon on the roof against the wall of the second story, positioning it against a protruding bracket. "Hurry, Hans," he whispered.

As Hans leaned his upper body through the window, the lights came on in the fireplace room. "The sound came from up here," a voice barked in German.

"Hurry, Hans!" Papa urged.

Hans scrambled through the window as fast as he could go. He grabbed the window casement to keep from sliding down the icy shingles. Papa quickly slid the window closed.

"Lie down on that side!" Papa ordered, dropping to a prone position on the western side of the roof. "Grab my arms to keep from sliding down and stay against the edge of the building! Maybe they won't spot us."

Hans dropped to his belly on the eastern side of the roof, gripping his father's arms to keep from sliding off. He pressed his body tight against the wall below the window. A light blinked on, casting a rectangle of light across the snow-covered roof. Less than a meter above them, the window slid open, and two officers leaned out into the blizzard.

Hans' heart pounded furiously as he and his father lay in the snow beneath the window, gripping each other's arms to avoid sliding down the incline of the roof. If the two Nazis looked down, they would be caught! Hans was thankful to realize that the moon had gone behind the clouds again.

"Check the safe!" a voice called from inside, and the two men closed the window and turned away. Hans let out a sigh of relief.

"Lie still," Papa whispered. "They may come back."

The snow continued to fall as Hans and his father clung to each other on the roof. The wind snarled and whipped the snow into their faces. Looking across the roof, Hans realized why the Nazis had not seen their tracks across the roof. The wind had already obliterated them.

Moments later, the roof was plunged into darkness as the lights inside blinked off. Papa pulled himself to a kneeling position, then straddled the peak of the roof, still gripping Hans by the arms the entire time. Hans pulled himself up to the peak of the roof, then leaned against the window ledge for support.

"Papa, look!" Hans whispered.

Down below, two Nazi soldiers came trudging through the snow around the corner of the building. Leaning their rifles against a tree, they both lit cigarettes.

Papa frowned. "*Monsieur* Blanc can't bring us the ladder as long as they're there," he whispered. "And we dare not stay here long." He reached down for the Joe Louis and, with great effort, managed to pull it up to balance it across the peak of the roof. Hans helped him hold it in place.

Papa began slowly to pull the rope up and coil it in his left hand. He pulled the grappling hook free from the roof, let the rope slide down the opposite incline of the roof, then set the grappling hook on the other side.

"Slide down the rope," Papa whispered, "but take it slow. Once you are down safely, I'll lower the cannon to you."

"What if the sentry sees us?" Hans whispered. "Once I drop over the edge, I'll be in full view of the hotel entrance."

Papa nodded. "It's a chance we'll have to take." He used his elbow to gesture toward the two soldiers. "I'm hoping that one of these men is the sentry."

Hans gripped the rope with both hands, lay flat on his belly, and began to slide down the roof. Moments later, he dropped safely into the snow. Papa pulled up the line, tied the rapid-fire cannon to it, and lowered it carefully to Hans. By the time Hans had untied Papa's knots, Papa had landed beside him.

"Let's go," Papa whispered. Stooping, he lifted the Joe Louis to his shoulder.

Papa hurried to the shelter of a hedge lining the hotel walkway and knelt beside it in the snow. Hans quickly joined him. Together, they silently scanned the yard and street, but all was silent. "Let's cut through the hedge and cross the walkway right here," Papa whispered. "Once we're through the second hedge, we'll be out of sight if those two soldiers come back around the corner. Follow me. Stay low, and move quickly."

Papa rose to a crouching position and pushed his way through a gap in the hedge. Hans was right behind him as he hurried across the walkway and forced his way through the hedge on the opposite side. Moments later, they slipped into the darkness of the street.

"Papa," Hans whispered, "the snow has stopped!"

Papa nodded. "We don't dare go back to *Madame* Benoit's house," he replied, "even if the soldiers weren't standing there. Our tracks would lead the Nazis right to her in the morning!"

"Where will we go?" Hans whispered.

"Let's head for *Monsieur* Marceau's place," Papa replied. "Perhaps we can get a message to Blanc to meet us there."

After walking down the street a hundred meters, Papa paused beneath a huge oak. "Help me get the Joe Louis into this harness," he said. "That will make it easier to carry."

Hans took the heavy weapon from him. Papa turned around, and Hans slipped the cannon into the loops of the harness, then tied the ends to it. At that instant, the moon came out again, bathing the quiet village in silvery white light.

Papa groaned. "This will make it easier for them to spot us," he worried. "I was thankful for the darkness."

Hans glanced toward the hotel. "Papa, look!" he said urgently.

A Nazi soldier stood in the hotel yard right at the very spot where Papa had lowered the Joe Louis to Hans! In the bright moonlight, Hans could see that the man's head was tilted back and that he was looking at the roof. "He found the rope!" Hans said.

As Hans and his father watched, the soldier reached up and gave a tug on the rope. He stepped back, looked up at the roof again, and then turned around and studied the hotel yard. Finally, he knelt in the snow.

"He's examining our tracks!" Papa said.

"And they lead right to us!" Hans replied.

The soldier stood to his feet and began to follow the tracks across the yard. He passed out of sight behind the hedge.

"He's on to us!" Papa declared. "Let's move!" He hurried down the street with Hans right on his heels. "We'll go right through town," Papa told Hans, "and try to mix our tracks with any others we find. Maybe we can throw him off our trail!"

Papa and Hans turned down a side street and ran as fast as they could go. At the next block they found a set of footprints leading west. "Walk in these prints!" Papa said, "But we have to hurry! We don't dare let him catch sight of us!"

A cloud crossed in front of the moon just then, and the street grew dark. Papa looked up gratefully. "Thank you, Lord," he breathed. "That will make it harder for him to see our tracks."

They followed the footprints past the church, where the trail crossed two other sets of tracks. Hans and Papa switched and began to walk in the new tracks. When they came to the mercantile, they found several sets of tracks and switched again.

"The problem is that the wind has partially filled in these footprints," Papa said. "When we walk in them, our prints are fresh and distinct."

The moon shone bright again as they left the village and headed up the hill toward *Monsieur* Marceau's house. Hans turned and looked down toward the village. His heart sank. The Nazi soldier held his rifle at the ready as he followed their trail in the snow.

19

THE INFORMANT

"Papa!" Hans exclaimed, "that Nazi is still on to us! He's following our tracks in the snow!"

Papa turned and gazed down the hill. "So he is," he said calmly. "Well, we'll just have to make it more difficult for him, won't we? If he likes our tracks so well, we'll make him some more!"

Papa dashed up the snow-covered slope until he reached the edge of the woods. Once inside the forest, he turned east and began to run between the trees, being careful to stay just inside the tree line. Hans struggled to keep up.

The fugitives followed the ridge until the woods dipped down into a valley. Papa paused, and Hans finally caught up. An icy stream splashed and gurgled over the slick rocks as it wound its way down to the village. "This will cover our tracks!" Papa declared. "But I warn you, it'll be cold!" He splashed right into the water.

Hans hesitated, then followed his father into the shallow water. The shock of the cold water was intense and took his breath away. The cold was so extreme that Hans felt a burning sensation in his feet and ankles. He sucked in his breath sharply, trying to overcome the pain.

"Watch your step!" Papa warned. "A slip in water this cold could be fatal!"

The little creek crossed a meadow, then ran along the southern edge of the village. Hans and Papa splashed along, moving as fast as they dared without taking a fall in the water. "How long do we have to stay in the water?" Hans pleaded.

"Untie the Joe Louis!" Papa urged. "I have an idea!"

Hans stepped behind his father, untied the knots, and slipped the heavy weapon from the loops. "Can you carry it for a moment?" Papa asked. "I need to untie the harness."

Hans carried the Joe Louis down the creek while Papa hastily slipped out of the harness. Papa's cold fingers fumbled at the knots. When he was finished, he had a straight rope six meters long with a large monkey-fist knot at the end. He coiled the rope and threw it over his shoulder, then took the cannon from Hans.

"We'll get out of the creek just around that next bend," Papa told Hans, "and circle back around to the bridge. I think we can lay a trap for our Nazi friend."

Hans glanced back along the creek. "He's gaining on us, Papa!"

"We'll have to hurry! Come on!"

Father and son hurried around the bend in the creek and scrambled up the bank. "Don't worry about leaving tracks," Papa said, as they left the water. "I want him to follow us." He chuckled. "But we'll make him wade the creek to get to us."

Hans followed his father in a large circle through a grove of trees until they came to a road. They followed the road back toward the bridge. Papa slowed down when they came in sight of the structure. "We'll keep walking until we get into the darkness of the bridge," Papa said, "but be ready to stop when I tell you to. I'll hand you the Joe Louis at that point."

Hans and Papa walked into the shadow of the covered bridge and started across. The bridge was dark. When they were halfway across, Papa suddenly stopped. "Here," he said, "take the Joe Louis."

Hans took the heavy weapon from his father. Papa tossed the knotted end of the rope up into the open rafters of the bridge. He pulled on the rope until he was sure that the end was caught securely, then climbed the rope into the darkness above.

"There's a slipknot loop in the end of the rope," Papa said a moment later. "Slip it around the Joe Louis, pull it tight, and let me pull it up."

He coughed once. "Listen carefully while you do that. We have to hurry. I want you to walk on across the bridge and keep on going until you get around the curve in the road. It's only fifteen meters or so. Once you are around the curve, step to one side, then walk backward to the bridge. Take big steps coming back. I want the soldier to see two sets of tracks leading away from the bridge."

"I understand," Hans said quickly. "Then what?"

"Once you are in the shadow of the bridge, slip around the end and crawl into the darkness under the bridge. Be careful not to leave tracks. And then, pray like you've never prayed before!"

"It's tied!" Hans said.

Papa pulled the Joe Louis up into the darkness of the rafters. "Go, Hans!" he said. "But hurry! That soldier will be along at any minute now."

Hans ran the rest of the way across the bridge and dashed through the snow around the curve in the road. Following his father's instructions, he jumped to one side, then began to run back toward the bridge, creating a second set of tracks. When he reentered the darkness of the bridge, he stepped around the corner and slid into the space beneath the timbers, being careful not to leave tracks. His heart pounded as he crouched beneath the bridge. Moments later, he saw the silhouette of the soldier approaching.

The Nazi paused as he neared the bridge. He glanced at the tracks in the roadway and then scanned the area around the bridge. Finally, he started across the darkened bridge. Hans crouched lower. The footfalls of the soldier echoed hollowly in the empty space beneath the bridge.

Hans heard a dull clank, then a loud thud, followed by a subdued thud. He slowly raised his head.

"He's out cold!" Papa said as he swung down from a rafter, then dropped to the floor of the bridge. "I'll get the Joe Louis. You get this guy's rifle and throw it in the creek."

Hans found the weapon in the darkness. He carried it to the end of the bridge and hurled it into the darkness below. A loud splash followed.

"Back into the water," Papa ordered. "We have to get out of here before he comes to."

Hans scrambled down the bank after his father. "What did you do to him?"

Papa laughed. "I just used the Joe Louis," he answered. "I dropped it on him." He chuckled. "Archer's right: it is an effective weapon."

They followed the stream back up into the woods, then stepped out on dry ground. Hans stomped his feet to try to restore circulation to his frozen toes.

"I think we're safe now," Papa said as they hurried down the road toward the village. "That soldier won't follow us without his rifle. And the wind's picking up again. It will obliterate our tracks before morning."

A horse nickered right behind them, and Hans spun around in alarm. Two horsemen were bearing down upon them. "Run, Papa!" Hans shouted.

"Von Edler!" a voice called. "Is that you?"

Hans sagged with relief. The voice belonged to *Monsieur* Blanc. "*Oui*, it's us," Papa answered.

"Did you get the Joe Louis?" Blanc asked anxiously.

"*Oui,* I have it right here," Papa replied.

"Give it to Marceau here," Blanc said. "We'll take it to St. Chamond tonight. Archer has a contact there that will get it back to the Allied air base safely."

Papa helped the men tie the rapid-fire cannon to the back of Marceau's saddle. He turned to Hans as the men rode swiftly down the hill. "Come on, let's get home and thaw out these poor feet of ours."

The next afternoon, Philipe and Hans hurried up the mountain trail toward the hidden hut to see Major Archer. Hans told his friend about the adventures he and his father had experienced the night before as they retrieved the rapid-fire cannon from the Nazi headquarters. Philipe was wide-eyed by the time the tale was finished. "Weren't you afraid?" he asked.

Hans nodded. "To be honest, I was terrified," he answered, "especially when the soldier locked onto our tracks like he did. But like Papa said, God was with us. I thought about that a lot, believe me. It was reassuring to know that if we were killed, we would go to heaven. I don't think I could have done it if I wasn't saved."

A sober look passed across Philipe's face, and Hans noticed it. "What's wrong, Philipe?"

"I was thinking about Colette," Philipe answered slowly. "Hans, she still doesn't know the Lord! Will you or Gretchen tell her how to be saved?"

"I talked with Gretchen about it," Hans replied. "She's a bit hesitant, but I think she's willing to try to talk with Colette. If she doesn't, I will."

"I want my sister to be saved, Hans," Philipe said seriously.

Hans nodded. "But I guess we're going to have to wait until your mother lets her out of the house again."

Philipe snorted. "I think she's been sneaking out when Mama and I are gone," he said. "I can't prove it, but . . ." He picked up a rock from the trail and hurled it through the trees, and then turned to face Hans. "Would Gretchen go to our house to talk to Colette?"

Hans shrugged. "I don't know."

"Colette will listen, Hans. She's not a bad person. She just . . ." Philipe fell silent.

"You know who I'd like to witness to?" Hans asked. "Major Archer! I don't know if he'd listen, because I'm just a kid, but he needs the Lord, too. I want to get a chance to talk with him about it, but I guess I'll have to wait until the other men aren't around."

Twenty minutes later, the boys entered the hut to find *Monsieur* Brisard with Major Archer. "Hello, boys," the pilot greeted them cheerfully. "Come on in! Hans, I hear that you had quite a night!"

Hans grinned. "It certainly wasn't boring."

Major Archer laughed. "Well, I want you to know that I'm proud of what you and your father did. The two of you are heroes! Oh, by the way, Blanc and Marceau sent word that the Joe Louis is safely back at my air base!"

"That's great, Major!" Hans declared. He struck his fist into his left palm to show his delight. "Thank God!"

The pilot nodded agreeably. "I guess you could say that. But really, you're the one who did it."

⇦ ⇨

Gretchen hurried up the steep mountain trail. "I wish Hans had waited for me!" she grumbled. "He knew I was almost ready to go! But no, he had to go rushing off with Philipe. They couldn't even wait five minutes!" She glanced back down the trail to be sure that she wasn't being followed, then stepped onto the tiny path that led to the hut.

As Gretchen neared the hut, she was astonished to see Colette Duval hurrying down the trail toward her. "Colette!" she gasped. "What are you . . ." She bit her tongue to keep from saying any more.

Colette laughed derisively. "I know your little secret," she gloated. "That American is in a little hut beneath the side of the hill! And I know where it is!"

Panic swept over Gretchen. "Colette! How did you find out?" There was no use in trying to trick Colette.

"I followed Philipe and Hans," the other girl smirked. "Boys think they're so smart! Well, they weren't smart enough for me!"

"What—what are you going to do?" Gretchen asked, frozen with fear.

"What do you think I'm going to do?" Colette retorted. "That man is a fugitive. I'm going to do what any good French citizen would do—I'm going to the authorities! In this case, that happens to be the Nazi commandant!"

"No!" Gretchen shrilled in horror. "They'll kill him! Colette, you can't!"

"Can't I?" Colette taunted. "Just watch me, Precious!"

Gretchen tried to grab Colette, but the taller girl deftly sidestepped. She flung Gretchen to the ground and ran down the trail.

20

THE TRAGEDY

Gretchen leaped to her feet. She had to do something. She couldn't stop Colette by herself.

Hans! He could stop her! Gretchen dashed to the hut and flung open the door.

"Hans!" She screamed. "She found it! She found it! She's going to tell! We have to stop her!" The words came in a torrent of tears.

Monsieur Brisard grabbed Gretchen by the shoulders. "Slow down," he said. "Start at the beginning. Now—who found what?"

"It's Colette!" Gretchen sobbed. "She found the hut! She followed Hans and Philipe up here, and she saw the hut. She's going to the Nazis right now!"

Hans leaped to his feet. "We'll stop her!" he declared.

Philipe grabbed his arm. "You'll never catch her in time, Hans. She's as fast as you are, and she knows these trails better than you."

He turned to Gretchen. "Where did you see her? Where?"

"Just this side of that giant oak that lies across the trail," Gretchen answered.

"Then she has a two-minute head start," Hans said. "We'll never catch her before she gets to the Nazi headquarters!"

Philipe grabbed Hans by the coat sleeve. "Wait!" he shouted. "There is a way! Come on!" He rushed to the door and then whirled around to face *Monsieur* Brisard. "Run down to the Nazi headquarters," he begged. "We'll need you to help with Colette! We'll try to hold her off until you get there."

Philipe leaped through the door of the little hut with Hans right behind him. "Hurry!" Philipe called as he raced down the narrow path.

Hans finally caught up with him as they reached the mining road. "Where are we going?" Hans gasped, trying to keep up. "What are we going to do?"

"The mining camp," Philipe answered over his shoulder. "I'll explain when we get there!"

Moments later the boys bolted around a curve in the road. Philipe scrambled over a gate blocking the road, and Hans followed him. Several small metal shacks sat in a clearing surrounded by rusting pieces of equipment. Two broken down trucks sat abandoned in the roadway, their tires rotting away. Philipe leaped over several power lines that lay across the ground. "The mine entrance is just beyond that rise," he said, pointing.

He ran to a shed and flung open the sagging metal door. "We found this just a month or two ago," he said. "It's our only way to beat Colette down to the village." As he said these words, he pulled a canvas harness and steel pulley from a pile of equipment.

Hans stared at him. "What are you going to do?"

"Come on!" Philipe replied. "There isn't time to explain."

Hans followed him to a pole tower nearly fifteen meters high at the lower edge of the camp. Looking up, Hans saw a steel cable leading from the tower across the treetops. "Follow me!" Philipe ordered, scrambling up the stairs in the center of the tower. Hans obeyed.

They came out on a tiny platform barely two meters across. From this vantage, Hans could see that the cable spanned the canyon in a shallow arc that ended at the foot of Mount Andriese on the other side of the village. Hans turned to Philipe in alarm. "No, Philipe! Don't do it! You don't know that it's safe!"

"It's only six hundred meters across," Philipe replied with determination as he opened the buckle on the harness. "And it's the only way to beat my sister to the village." He laid the pulley over the railing and held the harness open. "Here. Step in."

Hans recoiled in panic. "Me? Are you crazy?"

"You're the only one that can stop her in time," Philipe replied. He lowered his gaze. "She's stronger than me."

"But—but how do you know it's safe?" Hans sputtered. He eyed the thick cable over his head.

"It's the only way!" Philipe insisted. "Hurry!" He thrust the harness toward Hans, who reluctantly stepped into it. Philipe fastened the buckles around him. "Step up here."

As if in a daze, Hans stepped up onto a sturdy wooden platform. Philipe lifted the pulley assembly onto the cable and then fastened a bracket closed with a thumbscrew. The harness hung from two heavy canvas straps.

"This is your brake," Philipe told him, pointing to a chain that hung in front of his face. "But don't pull it until you cross the roof of the house behind the hotel. Hold your feet up!"

"Philipe, wait!" Hans said, but his friend had already shoved him clear of the tower. With a whirring, metallic scream, the pulley sped down the cable, carrying Hans with it.

The sickening feeling in the pit of his stomach as the cable carried him swiftly down and across the treetops turned into sheer terror as he left the mountainside and sped across the empty void of the canyon. He gulped a deep breath and tried to relax. The cable was holding him! He mustered the courage to look down.

Hans realized that he had just crossed over the canyon trail. He could see it snaking down the mountainside at the edge of the canyon, appearing to him as a thin, white line against the darker colors of the forest. Spotting movement on the trail below, he took a second look.

It was Colette, running full speed down the trail. She slowed slightly as she came to the treacherous place where the trail crossed the face of the cliff on the very brink of the canyon.

"Colette!" Hans shouted, his voice echoing across the canyon. "NO! Don't do it!"

Hans saw the girl look up at the sound of his voice. She slipped on the icy trail and tried in vain to recover her balance. To Hans' dismay, Colette tumbled over the edge of the precipice. Her scream of terror reverberated across the canyon as she fell. Hans turned away.

21

CAPTURE

The tower seemed to rush toward Hans with all the speed of an express train. Hans was in shock, overcome with horror at what he had just witnessed. He stared at the tower ahead, trying desperately to remember what he was supposed to do, but his mind refused to respond. His hand still held the handle to the brake chain, but he never pulled it.

Less than ten meters from the tower, a branch from a nearby tree rested across the cable. The pulley struck it at full speed.

The branch whipped to one side as the pulley sped past, and then snapped back. The impact knocked the pulley from the cable, causing Hans to lurch in the air. The pulley assembly spun over and over, jerking the brake chain from Hans' hand and wrapping the canvas straps around the cable. The resulting friction dragged the speeding pulley to a stop just as Hans' shoulder touched one of the tower poles. The tree branch had saved his life.

Hans took a deep breath and shook his head to clear his senses. He unfastened the buckles and freed himself from the harness, and then dropped in a bewildered heap on the tower platform. *Colette is dead,* he thought sorrowfully, *and we didn't even witness to her!* Bitter tears of remorse streamed down his cheeks.

Monsieur Brisard found him twenty minutes later. "Hans!" he said, scrambling up the short flight of stairs and hurrying to the boy's side, "Are you all right? Didn't you stop Colette?"

"Colette is dead, *Monsieur,*" Hans sobbed.

"Dead?" the man echoed. "What happened?"

It was Papa who was assigned the task of breaking the news of Colette's death to her mother and brother. As men from the village made their way to the canyon to retrieve her body, Hans and Gretchen, *Monsieur* Blanc, and *Monsieur* Brisard gathered in the Duval kitchen with Philipe and *Madame* Duval. Hans was unable to look Philipe in the eye.

Papa cleared his throat. "We have terrible news," he said gently, looking at *Madame* Duval, then at Philipe. "I wish there was an easier way to tell you, but there's not. There was a terrible accident this afternoon."

Madame Duval's hands flew to her mouth. "It's Colette!"

Papa nodded sadly. "*Oui, Madame.*" He paused. "She—was killed. I'm sorry."

Philipe dropped his head into his hands. "We didn't tell her," he sobbed. "We never told her about Jesus."

A cold feeling swept over Hans. He hung his head, trying to blink back the tears.

"Nail it!" Papa said as he held the brace in place on the new barn door. Hans quickly drove two nails in place at each end, and Papa released his grip. "Finish nailing it to the other planks, and then we'll take a short break," he said. "*Madame* Dubois should have lunch ready soon."

Hans reached for a nail. "I felt so sorry for Philipe yesterday when he heard that his sister had died," he said. "Did you see his face? I've never seen anyone so crushed! And it's my fault."

"Hold it," Papa replied. "Don't blame yourself. I'm sorry, too, that Colette was killed, but it's not your fault! She was planning to betray an Allied pilot to the Nazis, even though they are the enemies of her country! You did what was best."

Hans shook his head. "I'm not talking about that, Papa. Colette died unsaved. Philipe had asked Gretchen and me to tell her how to be saved, and we never did!" Tears suddenly welled up in his eyes and dripped down on the hammer. "If we had known she was going to be killed, we would have told her right away!"

Papa nodded sadly. "Life is short, and death often comes swiftly."

"Papa," Hans said, raising his head to look at his father, "I want to try to witness to Major Archer, before he leaves Messiere. I don't think he's saved."

Papa bowed his head. "You shame me, Son. I haven't even attempted to witness to the major."

Monsieur Blanc stepped around the corner of the new barn. "I need Hans and Gretchen," he said. "It's an emergency!"

Papa thrust his hammer into his tool belt. "What's wrong, *Monsieur*?"

"Major Archer got a message from RV4," Blanc answered. "The Germans are planning to interrogate everyone in the entire village in an all-out attempt to locate Archer. RV4 says we need to get him out today."

Hans caught his breath.

"We've been afraid of that," Papa said. He frowned. "I don't suppose that the Nazis know that we know?"

The villager shrugged. "We don't think so. But the important thing is to get Archer out of the region before the interrogation takes place. We're going to try to move him out today."

"What do you want Hans and Gretchen to do?"

"Doc Nilsson says that Archer is in no shape to walk yet," Blanc replied, "and we don't dare take a vehicle up; the Nazis would see it for sure. We're going to try to get him out on sleds."

Hans was puzzled. "How?"

"We'll carry him down to the mining road," Blanc said. "Once we reach the road, we face the greatest chance of discovery, so we'll use sleds from there."

"But it's far too steep!" Hans protested. "A sled would get going so fast it would sail right off the side of the mountain!"

"We borrowed three sleds from some of the village children," Blanc said. "Marceau is making a safety brake for each of them right now. You'll be able to control your speed."

"What do you want Hans and Gretchen to do?" Papa asked.

"We want them to make a run with the sleds," the man replied. "One of the teenage boys from the village will be on the third sled. We need to know if the sleds will make it all the way to the covered bridge before they run out of steam. Also, if the Nazis get suspicious and question them, it's just three young people having some fun.

"The second run will be Hans, Gretchen, and Major Archer. He'll be wearing the hat and coat that Marcel wore on the first run. RV4 will have an agent waiting with a vehicle at the bridge, and the two of them will get Archer safely out of the region."

Papa thought it over. "It sounds dangerous," he said finally, "but Von Edlers never run from duty. I'll talk to Gretchen."

Blanc pulled a watch from his pocket and glanced at it. "We need to hurry, *Monsieur*. The agents are to be at the bridge in ninety minutes."

Hans and Gretchen met Marcel and *Monsieur* Marceau behind the village church. Three wooden sleds with steel runners leaned against a nearby tree. Marceau took one of the sleds and set it on the ground.

"This is your brake lever," he told them, pulling on an iron handle just in front of the steering bar. "As you can see, pulling it up lowers this iron plate to drag the ground.

If you pull hard, this will bring you to a full stop within a few meters, even at full speed. To slow down for curves and such, just raise the handle part way. When you release the handle, the spring pulls it out of the way. You'll get the feel of it pretty quickly."

The three young people pulled the sleds up the steep mountain road. Four Nazi soldiers strode past in the opposite direction but didn't give the sleds a second glance. Hans was relieved when they had passed.

They reached a fork in the road, and Hans paused. "This is where we turn when we come down," he told the others. "This road will take us across the bridge. If we go straight, we end up in the center of town. But we'll have to watch for the turn."

They pulled the sleds all the way to the point where the road intersected the trail to the hut. They found *Monsieur* Blanc waiting for them.

"Make a run all the way to the bridge," he told them. "Holler and laugh on the way down. This has to look good for the Nazis. We'll have Major Archer waiting for you when you return."

Marcel threw himself on top of his sled and took off down the snow-covered road. Gretchen went next, with Hans bringing up the rear.

The snow-covered trees sped by as the sleds picked up speed. Hans drew back on the brake lever, and his speed dropped considerably. *Good,* he thought, *Marceau's brake works well!* A curve loomed unexpectedly in the road, and the sleds shot into it at full speed. But the riders braked hard and maintained control.

Hans allowed his sled to gain speed until he had passed Gretchen and came alongside Marcel. "Watch for the curves!" he shouted. "They come up fast!" Marcel nodded, and Hans dropped back behind Gretchen again.

In less than five minutes they had passed across the covered bridge. The riders braked to a stop a hundred meters beyond it. "We reached the bridge just fine," Hans declared. "I could have gone another five hundred meters easy."

The trio began the long trek back up the mountain. In spite of the cold, they were sweating profusely by the time they reached the trail to the hut. Papa and *Monsieur* Blanc rose from their hiding place in the bushes and helped Major Archer to his feet. The pilot exchanged coats and hats with Marcel.

"Any problems?" Blanc asked, as the men helped the pilot lie down on his sled.

Hans shook his head. "We made it past the bridge just fine."

"Hans, you take the lead on this run," Blanc instructed. "Take it just a bit slower. Major Archer hasn't been on his feet for a while. Gretchen, you bring up the rear. And I want you to whoop it up like you did on the first run."

Major Archer tested the brake lever, then raised his right hand to *Monsieur* Blanc. "*Merci, Monsieur.* You and your people have been lifesavers! I can't thank you enough for your help in saving the Joe Louis."

Blanc smiled. "It's been our pleasure."

Papa shook hands with the pilot, and then the ride began. Hans released his brake, and the sled shot forward. Seconds later, he glanced over his shoulder to see Major Archer and Gretchen speeding along behind him. He slowed for the first curve, then remembered to holler as Blanc had instructed.

Moments later, Hans slowed for a treacherous curve several hundred meters below the mining camp. The road was at its steepest and narrowest at that point, and the curve was sharp. As he swept into the turn, Hans braked hard and screamed, "Look out!" A Nazi jeep was barreling up the road toward them!

Pulling up on the brake handle with both hands, Hans managed to bring his sled to a stop just three meters from the front tires of the vehicle. Half a second later, Major Archer's sled slammed into his, throwing them both into the snow. Gretchen ground to a stop several meters from them.

"Are you all right, Major?" Hans whispered.

"*Oui*, I'm fine," the pilot replied.

They looked up to see a Nazi rifle pointed right at them. The soldier strode forward and yanked the bright red toboggan cap from the major's head. "The American!" he exclaimed. Turning to his companion in the jeep, he called, "We caught the American!"

"Let's get him into the jeep," the other replied. "I'll turn around at the mining camp!" The soldier climbed from the vehicle, picked up the sleds one by one, and hurled them over the side of the mountain.

Hans and Gretchen stood forlornly in the middle of the road, watching as the jeep climbed toward the mining camp. Major Archer lay helpless in the back.

Hearing a noise, Hans spun around to see a large man in a brown plaid jacket step from the woods. His heart leaped. "Help us!" he called. "The Nazis took Major Archer!"

The man ran toward them, and Hans' heart sank. The man was Klause, the retarded woodcutter!

22

RV4

Hans and Gretchen watched as the deaf man ran toward them. "Why did it have to be Klause?" Hans muttered. "I was hoping for someone who could help us!"

To their amazement, Klause reached into his coat and pulled out a machine pistol. "Quickly!" he ordered. "Into the woods! They'll be coming back in less than a minute!" His huge left hand held a grenade.

Dumbfounded, Hans stood and stared at the man. He finally found his voice. "We thought you were deaf!" he blurted. "But you're not! You're . . ."

"I'm an Allied agent," Klause replied. He pulled the pin from the grenade, scanned the road, and then hurled the grenade against the bank above the roadway.

An explosion shattered the stillness of the forest. The bank collapsed, blocking the road with a jumble of dirt and boulders.

Klause turned to Hans and Gretchen. "Get behind that log and stay down," he ordered. "The Krauts will be coming back in just a second, and I have to save Archer."

Hans and Gretchen scrambled to obey.

Twenty seconds later, the rumble of a motor told them that the jeep was returning. Hans raised up slowly. Klause was nowhere to be seen.

The jeep swept around the curve, then braked to a stop fifteen meters from the landslide. "Now what caused this?" the driver exploded. He set the brake and raised up over the windshield to take a better look.

"Hands over your heads!" a voice commanded in German. Klause suddenly appeared at the side of the vehicle with the machine pistol drawn. The soldiers obeyed.

"Step down from the vehicle without turning around," Klause ordered. "Now step forward three paces."

When the soldiers obeyed, Hans started to rise up from behind the log. Klause waved him back. "Stay down, Sergeant! I don't want them to see you! And don't speak!" Hans nodded and sank back behind the log.

The agent pulled a large bandana from his pocket and ripped it in half. He stepped up behind one of the soldiers and laid the barrel of the machine pistol against the back of the man's neck. "Follow orders, and I'll let you live," he said quietly. "Understand?"

Both men nodded.

"Remove your helmets slowly," Klause ordered, "and place your fingers under the webbing." The Nazis complied.

The Allied agent quickly blindfolded both men. He stepped to the jeep and found a coil of rope. Clutching the rope, he marched the soldiers into the woods. He returned in less than four minutes.

"Come out," Klause called to Hans and Gretchen, "but do not speak until I say so. Quick, now, I want you to get into the jeep."

Hans scrambled into the back of the vehicle with Major Archer, and Gretchen climbed into the front with Klause. The agent put the jeep into reverse and gunned the engine. The little vehicle backed up the steep road.

"We'll turn around at the camp and take another road down," the agent said. "You can speak now. Those soldiers didn't get a good look at you, and I didn't want them to hear your voices. They won't be able to identify you later."

"What did you do to them?" Hans asked.

"Just tied them to trees and gagged them," the agent replied. "We'll be out of here long before they work themselves free."

The jeep had reached the entrance to the camp, and Klause deftly turned it around and sped down another road. He glanced back at Major Archer. "You all right, Archer?"

The pilot nodded. "I'm fine, thanks to you. I do appreciate the rescue. But who are you? You look familiar!"

Klause laughed. "Don't remember, huh, Archie? Memphis High? You played center, and I played linebacker."

Major Archer stared. "Wysong? Charlie Wysong?"

The huge man laughed. "Glad you remember, Archie!"

Hans looked from one man to another as the jeep bounced down the steep road. "You two know each other?"

Klause nodded. "We're both Americans. We attended high school together."

Gretchen studied Klause's face. "You're RV4, aren't you?"

Hans' mouth fell open.

The agent laughed at the question. "Keep it under your hat, will you?"

Major Archer shook his head. "This is incredible!" he said. "RV4 turns out to be my old buddy, Charlie Wysong! Who would have believed it?" He glanced at the agent. "You've built quite a reputation for yourself, Wysong!"

A light came on for Hans. "You're the one who threw the grenade at the jeep the day that Major Archer was shot down," he told Klause. "And you're the one who got us the combination for the safe!"

Major Archer leaned forward. "Just how did you manage that, Wysong? I don't care if you are the legendary RV4; that was nothing short of a miracle!"

The agent grinned. "The safe was right beside my wood pile," he replied, "so it was a simple matter to see the combination to the safe. The Nazis thought that I was deaf and mentally retarded and did nothing to protect their secrets from me."

"But how did you know we even needed the combination?"

"Your little hut is built at the edge of a cavern," the agent responded. "I found another way into the cavern. Once inside, I could overhear everything you said. I'm not deaf, you know!"

"Why didn't you get the Joe Louis out of the safe?" Hans asked. "Wouldn't it have been easier for you?"

"I would have taken a chance on blowing my cover," the agent replied. "When I heard you discussing plans to do it, I left it in your hands. If you had failed, I would have stepped in and chanced it."

"I just have one more question," Major Archer said. "What were you doing in this region of France?"

"I was on another assignment that I'm not at liberty to discuss," Klause answered, "but it panned out just about the time you parachuted in. I simply stayed on to help."

The jeep braked to a stop at the base of Mount Piedler. "Better hop out here, Sergeant," Klause said. "And your sister, too. We appreciate your help."

"Be careful," Hans advised. He and Gretchen scrambled from the vehicle.

"Don't worry," the agent replied. "Sitting in that vehicle yonder are two of the best agents on God's earth. If the three of us can't get Archie back to base safely, nobody can!"

Major Archer held out his hand, and Hans shook it gravely. "*Merci*, Hans and Gretchen. I appreciate you both."

"We'll miss you," Gretchen replied. She looked at the secret agent. "We'll miss you too, Klause, even though we didn't get to know you very well."

Hans and Gretchen stepped into the woods and watched as the jeep sped toward the covered bridge. The vehicle disappeared from view as it pulled onto the bridge.

Moments later, a dark sedan emerged from the other end of the bridge and sped away.

"Well, he's safely away," Hans remarked.

"And RV4 as well," Gretchen answered.

Hans suddenly stopped cold. "Gretchen! We didn't get the chance to witness to Major Archer! And now he's gone forever!"

"Maybe not," his sister replied. "Several days ago he gave me his mother's address in America. He said I could write him there if I wanted."

Hans smiled. "We'll start a letter tonight," he declared. "Come on, I'll race you back to the farm!"

GLOSSARY

*Anschluss (Ger.)-(*AN schloos*)* the forced union of
       Austria with Germany by Hitler in 1938
Auf Wiedersehen`(Ger.)-(owf VEE der zayn) good-
bye
Bonjour (Fr.)-(bo ZHOOR) good-day, hello
Cassoulet (Fr.) –(ca soo LAY) stew
Danke schön (Ger) –(DAHN kuh shayn) many
thanks
Herr (Ger.) –(HEHR) sir, Mr.
Ja (Ger.) –(yah) yes
Knabe (Ger.) –(KNAH buh) by
Madame (Fr.) –(muh DAHM) Mrs.
Mademoiselle (Fr.) –(mah mo SEHL) Miss
Merci (Fr.) –(mare SEE) please
Monsieur (Fr.)-(me SYUR) Mr.
Nein (Ger.) –(Nine) no
Oui (Fr.) –(we) yes
Tout de suite (Fr.) –(toot sweet) quickly
Unteroffizier (Ger.) –(UNTR off fits eer) German
officer, equivalent of sergeant